Disney

FRIENDSHIP STORIES

Disney PRESS

New York

TABLE OF CONTENTS

DISNEY'S

Lilo & Stitch

Friends Forever

On a distant planet, a blue creature named Experiment 626 stood before the Grand Council. His creator, Jumba Jukiba, was with him. Because 626 destroyed everything he touched, Jumba had been accused of creating a monster.

The Grand Councilwoman turned to 626. "Show us there is something inside you that is good," she said.

"*Meega, na la queesta!*" replied 626.

"So naughty!" the Grand Councilwoman gasped. "It has no place among us. Take it away!"

Experiment 626 was put on a spaceship that would drop him off on a distant planet. But before he reached his new home, he escaped in a police cruiser. He headed straight for Earth—and the tiny island of Kauai.

The Grand Councilwoman sent Jumba and an Earth expert named Pleakley to retrieve 626.

Meanwhile, on the island of Kauai, a little girl named Lilo ran as quickly as she could. She was late for her hula class.

When she arrived, Lilo scurried into line, leaving a trail of saltwater behind her. The other dancers slipped on the wet floor and toppled over.

"Stop!" yelled her teacher. "Lilo, why are you all wet?"

She explained how she had dived into the water to feed a fish a peanut butter sandwich.

"You're crazy," said Mertle, one of the dancers.

Lilo pounced on her.

"Lilo!" yelled her teacher, pulling her away.

"I'm sorry," said Lilo. "I'll be good."

DISNEY FRIENDSHIP STORIES

But no one wanted Lilo to stay, so she went home. Lilo was very lonely. She didn't have any friends; her parents were gone; and her big sister, Nani, though a good big sister, was having a hard time learning how to be a parent. To top it all off, a social worker was threatening to take Lilo away from Nani.

That night, the sisters got in a huge fight. Lilo went to her room and slammed the door shut. Nani went upstairs and apologized.

Suddenly, Lilo saw something flash in the night sky. "A falling star!" she cried. "Get out, I have to make a wish."

Nani went into the hallway but stayed by the door so she could hear her sister's wish.

"I need someone to be my friend," Lilo whispered.

Nani hadn't realized how lonely her little sister was. Tomorrow, she decided, they would get a dog to keep Lilo company.

The flash Lilo had seen was Experiment 626's ship crashing on the island. A trucker found him and took him to an animal shelter. All the other animals were scared of 626, but he didn't care. He scrunched two of his four arms in toward his torso so he would look more like a dog. That way, he'd be adopted and have a place to hide from the aliens who were chasing him.

Lilo and Nani soon arrived at the shelter.

"Hi!" Lilo said when she saw 626.

"Hi," the creature replied, and then gave her a hug.

She walked back to the front room and told Nani she'd found the dog she wanted. "He's good," she said. "I can tell. His name is . . . Stitch."

They took Stitch home even though Nani thought he looked strange.

Nani was glad Lilo finally had a friend. When she left for work, Lilo and Stitch went for a ride. They rode all around the island, even stopping for ice cream along the way. Stitch was wild, but he and Lilo had fun.

Later, at the restaurant where Nani worked, Stitch spotted Jumba and Pleakley, who were dressed as tourists. When the aliens tried to capture Stitch, he almost bit Pleakley's head off. Nani's manager was furious and fired her. It was just the kind of thing Lilo and Nani didn't need.

At home, Stitch also began to tear things apart.

"We have to take him back," Nani said.

"We adopted him!" Lilo cried. "What about *'ohana?* Dad said *'ohana* means family! Family means—"

"Nobody gets left behind," Nani finished. "I know." She remembered how welcoming her parents had been, and how important family was to them. She changed her mind. She would give Stitch another chance—for Lilo's sake.

That night, while Lilo was sleeping, Stitch found a book called *The Ugly Duckling*. He looked through it and noticed that the duckling was by himself a lot, just like him.

He woke up Lilo and showed her the book. She explained that the duckling was sad because he didn't fit in. Stitch knew how that felt. He wanted to feel like he belonged somewhere, too.

Lilo decided to show Stitch how to be good so that he would fit in. First, she tried to teach him hula dancing. He did pretty well until his twirls got a little out of control.

Then, they tried the ukulele. At first, Stitch was rather good. But all of a sudden, he began to play the instrument like a heavy metal guitar and *smash!*—all the windows around him shattered.

Finally, Lilo took him to the beach. Here, she decided, he could show everyone what he had learned and how good he could be. Stitch grabbed his ukulele and waddled to the shoreline in front of all the tourists. He began twanging away.

The tourists loved the music and swarmed around him, taking pictures. But the flashes were too bright for Stitch. He grabbed a camera and smashed it to bits. A man soaked him with a squirt gun. The blasts of water made Stitch angrier. He grabbed the tourist and hurled him through the air. Everyone ran away as fast as they could. They were frightened.

Lilo was upset. Stitch hadn't learned to be good. Plus, the social worker saw what had happened and was worried about Lilo's safety.

15

That night, Lilo decided to talk to Stitch. "Our family's little, now," she told him. "But if you want, you could be part of it."

But Stitch knew he had made life harder for Lilo and Nani. He turned toward the window.

" '*Ohana* means family," Lilo continued. "Family means nobody gets left behind. But if you want to leave, you can."

Stitch climbed out the window and headed into the night.

When Lilo woke up, she told her sister that Stitch had left. "It's good he's gone," she said, trying not to sound upset. "We don't need him."

"Lilo," Nani consoled her, "sometimes you try your hardest, but things don't work out the way you want them to. Sometimes things have to change . . . and maybe sometimes they're for the better." Then she left to look for a job.

Meanwhile, Jumba had found Stitch and was chasing him through the forest. Stitch realized he didn't want to leave, after all—Lilo was his friend. He ran back to the house.

When Lilo saw him, she knew she had to help. "What are we going to do?" she asked.

Together, they fought Jumba, but it was a losing battle. In the process, the aliens destroyed Lilo and Nani's house. Lilo ran into the forest, devastated. Stitch followed her.

"You ruined everything!" she told him.

Just then, Captain Gantu, another alien sent to capture 626, trapped them and put them in a containment pod on his ship. Stitch escaped, but the ship took off—with Lilo inside!

Stitch knew he had to save Lilo. She was the only friend he had in the entire galaxy. He found Nani, and then he convinced Jumba and Pleakley to help them rescue Lilo. They fired up the police cruiser and raced after her.

When they got close to Gantu's ship, Stitch jumped out of the cruiser. He landed on the windshield and crawled toward Lilo. But Gantu managed to shake him off.

Lilo saw her friend. "Don't leave me, okay?" she cried.

"Okay," he replied.

Stitch managed to get back to Gantu's ship. He climbed through the windshield, threw Gantu off, and rescued Lilo.

"You came back," she said.

"Nobody gets left behind," he replied. He finally understood how important family was.

With Lilo in his arms, Stitch leaped onto the cruiser as Nani, Jumba, and Pleakley flew by.

They went to the beach where the Grand Councilwoman was waiting to take Stitch home. "This is my family," Stitch said, pointing to Lilo and Nani. He was allowed to stay on Earth, and the social worker decided not to take Lilo away from her sister.

Lilo and Stitch hugged each other happily. They knew they would be friends forever.

Walt Disney's
101 DALMATIANS

Friends to the Rescue!

In a townhouse in London, there lived two dogs named Pongo and Perdita who loved each other very much. Their human pets, Roger and Anita, and a cheerful housekeeper named Nanny, lived with them, too. They were all very happy together. Everyone got excited when they learned Perdita was expecting puppies.

"*Fifteen* puppies!" Roger exclaimed, on the stormy October night they were born.

Pongo beamed. He was filled with pride and love. Outside, lightning flashed and thunder roared. *Boom!*

Suddenly, the front door swung open, revealing a tall, thin woman wrapped in an enormous fur coat. She was Cruella De Vil, an old classmate of Anita's. She had heard that puppies were on the way and had come to buy them. She stroked her fur coat, grinning evilly. "I'll take them all!" she cried. "The whole litter!"

Pongo barked. He didn't like Cruella at all. He decided his puppies would never belong to her.

"I'm afraid we can't give them up," Anita told her.

Cruella glared at Roger and Anita and pulled out her checkbook and pen. "Don't be ridiculous . . . I'll pay you twice what they're worth!" She shook the pen so hard that ink flew all over Roger and Pongo.

Roger was annoyed. With Pongo by his side, he declared, "We're not selling the puppies!"

Cruella stormed out the door. "I'll get even. Just wait. You'll be sorry, you fools!"

Weeks passed, and the puppies grew strong and healthy. Each night, Patch, Lucky, Rolly, and the others snuggled while Pongo and Perdita took their pets for a walk.

One night, while Pongo, Perdita, Roger, and Anita were out, two evil men named Jasper and Horace went to the Dalmatians' home. They pushed past Nanny and stole the puppies.

"Police! Help!" cried Nanny when she realized what had happened. But it was no use. The police couldn't find the puppies. When Roger and Anita returned, they were horrified. They didn't know what to do.

"It's all up to us," Pongo told Perdita. Roger and Anita were only human, after all. The Dalmatians decided to use the Twilight Bark. One dog would howl a message, then the next dog would pass it along, and so on. It was the quickest way for dogs to send news across the country.

The next night, Pongo and Perdita led Roger and Anita to the top of a windy hill in the park. Pongo barked and barked, sending news about the stolen puppies.

There was no answer. "I'm afraid it's too cold," Perdita said, shivering. "There's no one out tonight!"

Then, in the distance, a faint bark sounded. Danny the Great Dane had heard the news: fifteen Dalmatian puppies stolen! It was an all-dog alert.

Soon, the news spread to dogs all over the city . . . to a Scottish terrier in the street . . . to an Afghan in a window . . . to a poodle in a fancy car. From pet shops to homes, from rooftops to alleyways, the dogs of London passed the message along.

They would do whatever they could to help find the missing pups.

The barking reached the edge of London, then beyond. On a grassy knoll past a long, wide creek, an old dog named Towser listened. Then he barked the message to a nearby farm.

Inside the barn, a sheepdog named the Colonel perked up his ears. "Fifteen spotted puddles stolen," he told his friend, a cat named Sergeant Tibs. "Two woofs, one yip, and a woof."

"It sounds like puppies, not puddles," the cat said. Then Tibs remembered he'd heard barking at the old De Vil place two nights ago. The missing puppies had to be there.

The Colonel and Tibs snuck over to the abandoned castle and spotted the pups. "One . . . two . . ." Tibs began to count. The fifteen stolen puppies *were* there—along with eighty-four others!

Cruella De Vil had gotten Jasper and Horace to kidnap the Dalmatian puppies so she could use their fur to make coats!

The Colonel barked the news that he'd found the missing puppies to Towser, who sent it to Danny, who howled to Pongo and Perdita. "The puppies have been located somewhere north of here," the Great Dane told them. "I'll go along with you as far as Camden Road."

Together, they traveled to the city's edge. The Great Dane pointed the way. "Contact old Towser. He'll direct you to the Colonel, and the Colonel will take you to your puppies at the De Vil place."

"De Vil!" Pongo and Perdita exclaimed. They knew they had to get to their puppies quickly—Cruella was not to be trusted.

Pongo and Perdita plodded through the snow. After a while, they met Towser, then headed toward the Colonel.

Meanwhile, inside the De Vil place, Sergeant Tibs was helping the puppies escape. They hurried through a hole in the wall and down some steps.

The pups hid under the stairs, but soon Horace and Jasper discovered them. As the evil men crept toward the puppies, Pongo and Perdita crashed through the window. The two dogs bared their teeth, and leaped onto Cruella's thugs. The men fell to the floor.

Sergeant Tibs led the puppies back to the Colonel's barn while Pongo and Perdita fought Jasper and Horace.

Soon, the puppies were reunited with their parents. Pongo nuzzled them. "Is everybody here?" he asked.

"Now there's ninety-nine of us!" cried Patch.

Pongo and Perdita decided to take all ninety-nine puppies back to London to keep them safe from Cruella. But they'd have to move quickly to stay ahead of her.

"We'd better run for it," said Pongo.

"How can we ever repay you?" Perdita asked Sergeant Tibs and the Colonel.

"All in the line of duty," the Colonel replied.

The Dalmatians scampered away just as the thugs arrived at the barn. Their journey was difficult. The puppies kept slipping on the ice. It was very cold, and London was so far away.

"I'm tired and I'm hungry, and my tail is frozen," Lucky whimpered. He sat down, unable to go any further.

Pongo lifted his son by the scruff of his neck. But he and Perdita couldn't carry all of the pups. How would they make it?

Just then a collie ran up to the Dalmatians. "Pongo," he said, "we have shelter for you!"

The dogs from the Twilight Bark had come up with a plan!

The collie led the Dalmatians to a dairy farm, where friendly cows provided milk, and the puppies rested in the soft hay.

The collie even brought them some table scraps to eat. "It might hold you until Dinsford," he said. "There's a Labrador there."

Perdita yawned. All the animals had been so helpful. "I don't know what we'd have done if . . ." she trailed off, already asleep.

The next morning, Cruella joined the search for the puppies. By the time the Dalmatians reached Dinsford, she and Horace and Jasper weren't far behind.

Pongo and Perdita led the puppies to a blacksmith shop, where a Labrador was waiting. "The van down the street? It's going to London," the Labrador said. Pongo and Perdita were delighted. That meant they would be able to ride the rest of the way home.

Just then, Cruella's car screeched to a stop next to the van.

Pongo and Perdita didn't know how they'd be able to get the puppies to the truck without Cruella noticing them . . . until Patch and Lucky rolled past, covered in soot from the fireplace.

Pongo gazed at the pups. Then he jumped into the soot, turning himself brown from head to tail. "Look, I'm a Labrador!"

One by one, the puppies dove into the ashes. Soon, they were completely covered. They trotted outside and got into the truck—right under Cruella's nose. She was looking for Dalmatians, not Labradors!

But just as Pongo rounded up the last group of puppies, some snow fell on one of them. The soot came off, revealing white fur.

Cruella could tell the puppy was a Dalmatian. "After them!" she shouted.

The thugs leaped forward. But the Labrador raced up, growling. The men stopped in their tracks, leaving Pongo enough time to grab the last puppy before the truck left for London.

Cruella raced after the moving van, trying to run it off the road. Horace and Jasper sped toward it, too. But the driver turned just in time.

Crash! Cruella's car collided with the thugs' truck. They careened out of control, rolling over the side of the hill.

"You idiots! You fools!" Cruella screamed as the Dalmatians' truck drove on to London.

Before long, Pongo and Perdita brought the puppies to their townhouse. Roger and Anita were delighted to see them, and Nanny helped dust them off.

All one hundred and one Dalmatians were safe at home with their pets. And it was all thanks to the friends they'd met along the way.

Walt Disney's DUMBO

Dumbo Takes Flight

"Isn't he cute!" the lady elephants cooed when the baby elephant was delivered to the circus train. "Isn't he a darling?" Mrs. Jumbo beamed with pride at her new son, Jumbo Junior.

"*Ah . . . ahh . . . choo!*" The baby elephant sneezed. His whole body shook, and his ears suddenly uncurled. They were huge—much bigger than a normal elephant's ears. The lady elephants gasped and shook their heads in disapproval. "Just look at those ears!" they said.

"Precious little Jumbo," one lady elephant said mockingly.

"Jumbo? You mean Dumbo!" another cried. They all laughed. From that day on, everyone called the little elephant *Dumbo*.

Mrs. Jumbo ignored them. As far as she was concerned, her son was perfect.

Soon, the train arrived in town. Once the equipment was unloaded and the tents were pitched, the circus parade began! A band played merrily and crowds cheered as the animals marched through the streets. Dumbo followed his mother, but his ears were so big that he tripped over them and fell into a mud puddle!

A bunch of kids jeered at the little elephant and began to taunt him. They pulled his ears so hard that Dumbo fell over when they let go!

Mrs. Jumbo was furious. She picked up a bale of hay and threw it to the ground. The people who ran the circus were worried she might hurt someone, so they put chains around her and locked her in a circus wagon—by herself.

Heartbroken, Dumbo sat in a corner and cried. The other elephants snickered. It was all his fault, they decided. "Yes, him with those ears that only a mother could love," one of them said.

When Dumbo walked by, the other elephants pretended not to see him. Nobody wanted to talk to him. The baby elephant was all alone.

Luckily, Timothy Q. Mouse was sitting nearby. "Poor little guy!" he said to himself. "There he goes, without a friend in the world." The mouse decided to help. He sneaked up to the elephants. "You like to pick on little guys, huh?" he shouted. "Well, why don't you pick on me!" The elephants ran away quickly—they were all scared of mice.

Dumbo was afraid of the mouse, too. He hid in a haystack. Timothy tried to coax him out. "Look, Dumbo," the mouse said, "I'm your friend! Come on out!" But the little elephant just shook his head.

Timothy finally got Dumbo to come out by offering him a peanut and some promises. He told Dumbo he'd help him find his mother again. First, though, he was going to come up with a circus act for the little elephant.

The ringmaster decided to try something new the next night: a pyramid of elephants. Timothy convinced him to make Dumbo the grand finale. The young elephant was supposed to jump on a springboard and catapult to the top of the pyramid.

When Dumbo tried it, though, he smashed into the bottom of the pyramid, causing the rest of the elephants to tumble to the ground and the circus tent to collapse.

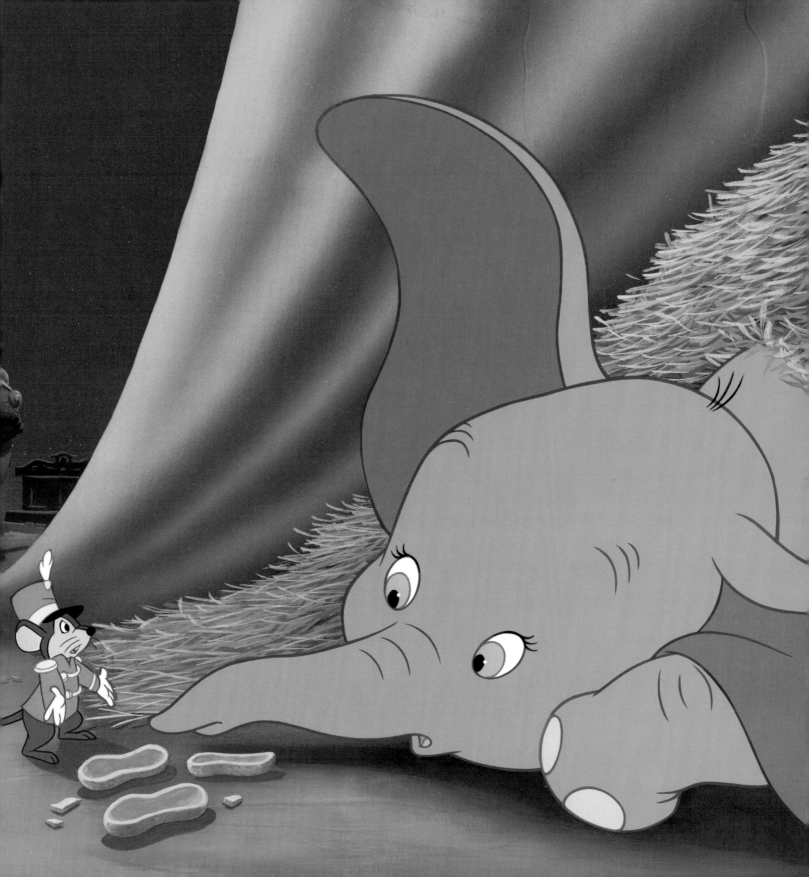

The elephants were bruised, bandaged, and embarrassed. They couldn't wait to get back at Dumbo. But the ringmaster was angry at him, too. He decided to make the little elephant into a clown.

The other clowns painted Dumbo's face and dressed him like a baby. They even made him wear a diaper. As flames leaped up all around him, the clowns pretended to rescue him from a burning building. They even threw water in his face! As if that wasn't bad enough, the clowns then pushed him off a tall tower and into a tub of plaster. The audience loved the act—but Dumbo felt ashamed.

After the show, Timothy tried to cheer up the elephant. "You're a big hit!" he announced. "You ought to be proud!"

Dumbo just looked at the ground. If this was what being a star was like, he didn't want any part of it.

Timothy stood on a cake of soap and helped the elephant clean the makeup off his face. "Come on!" he nudged his friend. "I gotta wash behind your ears!" Dumbo barely managed to smile.

Before long, big tears trickled down Dumbo's face. Timothy didn't know how to make his friend feel better. Then he thought of something. He snapped his fingers. "I forgot to tell ya. We're going over to see your mother!"

46

The mouse led Dumbo to the wagon where Mrs. Jumbo was tied up. The baby elephant stood on his hind legs and peered in anxiously at his mother. Mrs. Jumbo tried to come to the window, but the chains held her back. Luckily, her trunk fit between the bars. She scooped her baby up and rocked him, soothing him with a lullaby. Dumbo felt safe and peaceful.

When it was time to say good-bye, mother and son held on to each other for as long as they could.

As he and Timothy returned to the tent, Dumbo began to cry. The mouse tried to comfort him. "We may've had a lot of hard luck up till now," Timothy said, "but you and me is gonna do big things together." Dumbo was still sad, but it was nice to have a friend who believed in him.

The next day, Timothy woke up and noticed that he and Dumbo were in a tree. He had no idea how they'd gotten there. While the elephant slept, the mouse tried to figure it out. "Now, let's see," he mused. "Elephants can't climb trees, can they? Naw . . . that's ridiculous! Couldn't jump up! Uh-uh, it's too high!"

A group of crows was sitting on a branch above them. "Hey there, son—maybe you all flew up!" the crow said.

Timothy laughed, then stopped. "That's it!" he cried. Suddenly everything made sense! Timothy grabbed one of Dumbo's ears and shouted, "Why didn't I think of this before? Your ears . . . they're perfect wings! The very things that held you down are going to carry you up!"

It took a while to convince Dumbo, though. But when Timothy handed him a feather and told him it had magical powers that would make him fly, Dumbo spread his ears and soared through the air!

Under the big top that night, Dumbo stood on the top of the burning tower, clutching his magic feather. He was about to surprise the whole circus with his flying. But when he jumped, the feather slipped! Dumbo plummeted toward the ground, paralyzed with fear. But Timothy urged him on, shouting, "The magic feather was just a gag! You can fly! Honest you can!"

Right before he hit the floor, Dumbo spread his ears. Maybe Timothy was right. Then the most amazing thing happened—he began to fly. He flew higher and higher, even doing loop-the-loops. The audience was amazed.

The next day, Dumbo made headlines in the newspapers. Soon, he was setting world records—and appearing in movies, too! Just as Timothy had predicted, Dumbo was a star!

None of the other animals dared to make fun of him now—
Dumbo was the circus's main attraction. He had his own car on
the circus train, even though he usually flew. But when Dumbo
needed a rest, he would stop to see his mother, who'd finally
been freed. And he always kept a special place in his heart for
his faithful friend, Timothy Q. Mouse.

Disney
Winnie the Pooh
The Best-Friend Sleepover

"Comfortable, Piglet?" Winnie the Pooh asked. The bear was tucking his friend into a dresser drawer that he had made into a little bed.

"Oh, yes, Pooh. Thank you ever so much," Piglet replied. "The bed is just the right size."

"Well, good night, then," the bear said, blowing out the candle and climbing into bed.

"Good night, Pooh Bear," Piglet replied. He and Pooh were having a best-friend sleepover. It had been lots of fun so far. First, they had enjoyed a before-bedtime snack. Then, they had put on their pajamas and made up a story.

Of course, it was always fun spending time with Pooh. But there was something about being here for bedtime that was so . . . so . . . different from being at his own house, thought Piglet.

As he lay in the dresser drawer, his eyes wide open, Piglet noticed that it seemed much, much darker here than it did at home.

"Pooh?" he called out softly. "Are you still awake?" He wanted to ask the bear if it was always so dark. When Pooh did not answer, Piglet realized that his friend must have fallen asleep.

Oh, well, Piglet thought as he rolled over and pulled up the covers. Then he closed his eyes tightly and tried to get to sleep.

After a while, Piglet opened one eye and peered out into the darkness. He hadn't been able to fall asleep yet. He noticed that it was very, very quiet in Pooh's room—much quieter than it was in Piglet's own room at night. The quiet that was coming from the direction of Pooh's bed, where Piglet's best friend was fast asleep while Piglet lay wide-awake—that was the quietest quiet of all.

"Pooh? Pooh Bear?" Piglet called out, a little louder this time. He didn't want to wake up his friend. But he wondered if perhaps the bear was awake and had just not heard him the last time he called. Maybe they could talk or sing a song. Then it wouldn't be quite so quiet. But Pooh didn't answer. I guess he really is asleep, Piglet said to himself.

Just then, the quiet was broken by a peculiar noise. Piglet sat up and listened closely.

At first, the noise was a soft, low rumbling—curiously similar to the sound of a sleeping bear who was snoring. As Piglet listened, the sound grew louder and louder . . . and then softer and softer . . . and then louder and louder . . . over and over again! What if a Heffalump was coming to get them? Piglet wondered. He began to tremble with fright.

"Pooh! Oh, d-d-dear!" Piglet shouted. He jumped out of the drawer and ran to his friend's bedside. He shook Pooh and shouted, "Wake up! Wake up! Oh, p-p-please, P-P-Pooh!"

"Hmm?" Pooh asked drowsily. Slowly, he climbed out of bed and lit a candle. He shone it everywhere—and noticed Piglet wasn't in his drawer. Then he spotted a large lump in his own bed. Piglet had hidden under the covers!

"Why, Piglet," said Pooh, "what's the matter? Why did you get out of bed?"

Piglet was trembling so much, he had a hard time speaking. "It's that horrible, horrible n-n-noise, Pooh," he stammered. Piglet listened for the noise so he could point it out to Pooh, then realized that it had stopped. "That's funny," said Piglet as he peeked out from under the covers. "The noise stopped as soon as you woke up."

"Hmm," the bear said, yawning. "I guess that means we can go back to sleep."

Piglet didn't think he'd be able to fall asleep.

"I don't mean to be a bad best friend," he said.

"But do you think we might have the rest of our best-friend sleepover some other night? I'm just not used to sleeping anywhere but my own house."

Pooh sat on the bed and put his arm around Piglet. "I understand," he said. "We can have the rest of our best-friend sleepover whenever you like." Pooh helped Piglet gather his things. Then, hand in hand, they walked through the Wood to Piglet's house.

"Here you are, Piglet," Pooh said as they entered. "Home, sweet home."

"Thank you so much for walking me here," Piglet replied. "I suppose you'll be needing to get home to bed now?"

Pooh thought for a moment. "Yes, but first I might sit down for a little rest." He eyed a comfortable chair. "Just for a few minutes."

While Piglet put away his things, Pooh sat down and put up his feet. Then he decided to rest his eyes, just for a moment.

By the time Piglet finished, Pooh was fast asleep. He was even making a soft, rumbling sound. But in the comfort of Piglet's own house, it did not sound scary like a Heffalump. It just sounded like a sleeping bear who was snoring.

Piglet covered Pooh with a small blanket and slipped a pillow under his head. "Sweet dreams, Pooh Bear," he whispered. Then Piglet climbed into his bed and drifted off to sleep.

Pooh and Piglet slept all night. The next morning, Piglet woke up and saw that his friend was still asleep. He woke up Pooh gently, and they had a yummy breakfast. It had been a wonderful best-friend sleepover, after all.

DISNEY's
POCAHONTAS

Friends in a New Land

High on a cliff, an Indian princess named Pocahontas was exploring the forest with her friends Meeko, a raccoon, and Flit, a hummingbird. Although the two creatures didn't always get along, both loved Pocahontas and were almost always with her.

Suddenly, Pocahontas's friend Nakoma called to her from the river. "Your father's back!" she shouted. "Come down here."

Pocahontas began to run through the forest, then turned and jumped off the cliff instead. She swan-dived into the crystal blue river and swam over to Nakoma's canoe.

Meeko leaped off the cliff after Pocahontas. He grabbed Flit nervously on the way down, and they dropped into the river with a splash.

Breathlessly, Meeko scrambled into the canoe, shook himself off, and took his usual lookout post at the front. Flit, annoyed at the raccoon for getting him wet, hovered in the air as Pocahontas and Nakoma steered the canoe home.

When they arrived back at the village, Chief Powhatan
was happy to see Pocahontas. "Kocoum has asked to seek your
hand in marriage," he told his daughter. "He will make a
good husband."

"But he's so serious," Pocahontas replied unhappily.

Meeko agreed. When Powhatan wasn't looking, the raccoon
puffed up his chest and made a grim face, pretending to be
Kocoum. The silly animal could always make Pocahontas laugh.

Still, the young woman was troubled. She
went to see the ancient tree spirit,
Grandmother Willow, to ask for her advice.
Pocahontas told her about a spinning
arrow she kept seeing in a dream.

"It is pointing you down your path,"
the wise spirit told her.

As Pocahontas tried to figure out what her path was, she climbed high into the branches of Grandmother Willow, with Meeko and Flit close behind. They saw something they'd never seen before: a large boat with sails that Pocahontas mistook for clouds. It was the *Susan Constant*, a ship filled with English settlers seeking gold.

A while later, Pocahontas saw one of the settlers exploring the forest. She was curious but cautious as she hid behind some bushes. However, Meeko was a very mischievous raccoon. He always thought with his stomach . . . and followed his nose. He scurried toward the man and poked his nose into the settler's bag.

"Well, you're a strange-looking fellow," said the man, who was named John Smith. "You hungry?"

He handed the raccoon a biscuit. Meeko nibbled happily.

Still hidden, Pocahontas smiled. She was glad to see this stranger being so generous to her friend.

Flit, on the other hand, was worried about Pocahontas. Even if Meeko had gotten them into this mess, the hummingbird would do his best to get them out of it. Ever protective, he flew straight at the newcomer, poking at him and trying to make him leave. Luckily, Smith got called away by one of the other settlers.

Soon, Pocahontas met John Smith face to face. As they got to know each other, she showed him how the land and water, the people and animals, were all connected to one another. John Smith was fascinated with all that Pocahontas had to teach.

Meeko was fascinated, too—with Smith's bag! The raccoon eagerly searched for more biscuits. But Flit, on the other hand, circled angrily around Smith's head.

"Flit just doesn't like strangers," Pocahontas explained to John Smith.

"Well, I'm not a stranger anymore," Smith said. He extended a finger to Flit, but the bird just poked it with his sharp beak.

"Stubborn little fellow, isn't he?" Smith said.

"Very stubborn," Pocahontas agreed.

Just then, Meeko popped out of Smith's bag. In his paw was a compass. It was too hard to eat, but Meeko hid his discovery in Grandmother Willow's branches anyway.

Meanwhile, at the settler's camp, Percy, a very spoiled dog, sat on a pillow, feeling lazy and looking smug. He was the pet pug of Governor Ratcliffe, who had been on the ship that brought the settlers to this new land. Percy had always had an easy life. His pillows were the finest and the fluffiest. And he was always given the most delicious food. He was one pampered pooch . . . until Meeko showed up!

The always-hungry raccoon had followed John Smith to his camp. It wasn't long before Meeko spied Percy's fine dinner. With a quick hand, he shoved it all into his mouth.

Percy was furious when he saw what the raccoon had done! Barking wildly, the dog ran after Meeko.

Percy chased him out of the camp and into the forest, near Grandmother Willow. Pocahontas and John Smith were there, too.

Smith had hurried back after learning that the settlers wanted to attack the Indians, and he and Pocahontas were trying to figure out how to keep the peace. They had realized how much the settlers and the Indians could teach each other.

Percy growled at Meeko and continued to chase him.

"Meeko!" scolded Pocahontas.

John Smith shook his head. "You see what I mean? Once two sides want to fight, nothing can stop them."

Nothing except Grandmother Willow. "All right, that's enough!" the ancient tree spirit said to the animals.

Percy was so stunned to see a talking tree that he fainted!

A bit later, Grandmother Willow dipped one of her branches into the river. It caused the water to ripple outward. She explained that although the ripples were very small at first, they quickly grew larger. "But someone has to start them," she said.

Pocahontas and John Smith knew that the tree spirit was trying to get them to change the way the Indians and the settlers felt about each other. They agreed to talk to Chief Powhatan to see if peace could be reached.

They never made it, though. Along the way, an Indian warrior attacked Smith. Then, another settler shot the warrior, but Smith took the blame. He was taken prisoner and led to the Indian village.

77

Flit, Meeko, and Percy watched the whole thing from the base of a tree. As Flit and Meeko began to follow Pocahontas back to the village, they turned and saw poor Percy, shaking with fear. Then the most surprising thing happened: Meeko laid a comforting paw on Percy's head, and the pug stopped shaking. With a nod, Meeko let Percy know he could come with them.

Back at the village, the new friends looked on with sadness as Pocahontas visited John Smith. The Indians had decided he would die the next morning.

"I'm so sorry!" she cried. "It would have been better if we'd never met. None of this would have happened."

"Pocahontas, I'd rather die tomorrow than live a hundred years without knowing you," John Smith told her.

Pocahontas was heartbroken. She went back to see Grandmother Willow. "What can I do?" she asked sadly.

Meeko wanted to help his friend. Trying to cheer up Pocahontas, he handed her John Smith's compass, which he had hidden.

Looking at it, Pocahontas saw the spinning arrow that she had dreamed about.

Now she knew what path to follow. Quickly, she ran to the village and stepped in front of John Smith, willing to give up her life to protect him.

Chief Powhatan laid down his weapon, but the settlers had arrived. Governor Ratcliffe fired his gun.

"No!" yelled Smith. He jumped in front of the Indian chief, taking the bullet himself.

John Smith knew he would have to return to London to have his wounds treated. He and Pocahontas said good-bye, and he was carried to the ship. Everyone was sad to see him go.

Percy decided to stay in the new land with Meeko and Flit, and they were happy to have him around. They watched as John Smith sailed away, thinking about how much had happened and what a wonderful surprise their new friendships turned out to be.

Blueberries on Parade

Francis the ladybug rested in a bed in the ant infirmary. He had hurt his leg rescuing Princess Dot from a bird.

The princess had already visited him once to thank him. Now she was back and had brought the other members of her Blueberry troop along.

"To honor you, we've added spots to our bandannas," said her friend Teeny.

"And guess what else?" exclaimed Dot. "We want you to be our honorary Blueberry troop den mother!"

Francis scowled. Dot and the other Blueberries thought he was a female because he was a *lady*bug.

"Wait a second!" he cried. What did he know about watching a bunch of girls?

Just then, Dr. Flora came in. "Run along, girls. The patient needs to rest. You can visit him later on."

"Awww, that's too bad," Dot said. "Don't worry, we'll be back to visit soon, Den Mother." With that, the Blueberries left.

A few days later, Dot and two of the Blueberries returned to Francis's room. They couldn't seem to stop giggling.

The ladybug sighed. "How did I get stuck with this job?" he wondered.

Dot raised her hand. "May I start the meeting?" she asked. "I have something important to say."

"Yeah, all right," Francis muttered.

"We have another big surprise for you, Den Mother," began
Dot. "To thank you and the other circus bugs for all that you've
done, we are going to put together a parade! It'll be
the best ever."

"And we want *you* to help us," Teeny added.
"Right, girls?"

"Right!" the other Blueberries answered
enthusiastically.

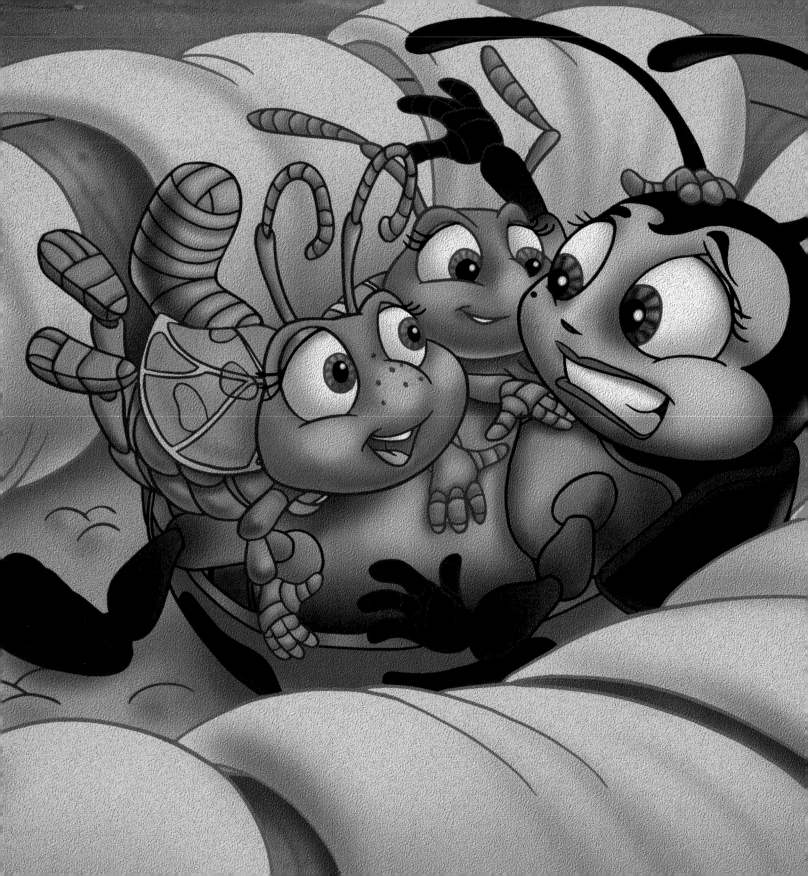

Oh, great, thought Francis.

"Well, girls," he said, "why don't you go outside and get started? I'll just take a little rest and join you later, okay?"

"Okay!" the Blueberries cheered. Then they rushed over to give him a hug.

"Watch out for my leg!" the ladybug cried.

The girls piled onto his cast.

"*Yeowww!*" Francis shouted. "My leg!"

"Oops! Sorry, Den Mother," said Dot. She and the other Blueberries tried to make him comfortable again.

"We've never held a parade before," Dot said. "What do we do first?"

Francis tried hard to be patient. "Why don't you start by making a flag? Outside!"

"Thanks for the great idea!" exclaimed Dot. "We'll work on it at our meeting tomorrow."

The next day, the Blueberries gathered to talk about the parade.

They decided to march from the Blueberry clubhouse to the banquet hall. There, the parade would end with a big party.

But the hardest part would be making the flag. They wanted it to be perfect to please Francis.

None of the designs they came up with seemed quite right, though.

88

"I know!" Dot suggested finally. "Let's each make a special decoration to put on the flag."

"That's a great idea!" Teeny exclaimed. "It'll make the flag extraspecial."

The other Blueberries loved the idea. Soon they were sticking flower petals, pebbles, and leaves on the flag with tree sap.

They worked all afternoon. "It looks pretty good," Dot said when they had finished.

The Blueberries were getting ready to show the flag to Francis when—*splat!*—a chunk of berry hit it. Juice dripped all over the flag.

"What's happening?" cried Dot.

Splat! Another red glob hit the flag. *Splat! Splat! Splat!* Berries flew through the air and landed on the flag. Soon, it was covered with splotches of red. The Blueberries looked at their creation with dismay. All of their hard work—and their gift to Francis—had been destroyed.

Suddenly they heard laughing. They turned to see a group of boy ants grinning at them. It was the Boysenberry troop! The boys turned and ran away.

"Those mean boys!" exclaimed Teeny. "They always ruin everything. Now what are we going to do?"

"Let's go ask our den mother!" Dot suggested. "He'll know exactly what to do."

A little while later, the Blueberries stood sadly around Francis's bed. They showed him their stained flag.

"We were trying to make something special for you," Dot explained. "But the Boysenberries ruined it!" She began to cry. Tears trickled down the cheeks of the other Blueberries, too.

The girls looked so upset, Francis couldn't help but feel sorry for them.

Maybe I can help them out a little, he thought.

"Okay, Blueberries!" Francis exclaimed. "You want to keep those Boysenberries out of your antennae?"

"Yeah!" cried the Blueberries.

"Then listen to your den mother!" Francis commanded. "If we all work together, we can still have the parade—and teach those Boysenberries a lesson!"

"All right!" the Blueberries cheered and jumped up and down.

Over the next few days, the Blueberries met with Francis. He helped them make a new flag. He also said they needed to get ready in case the Boysenberries attacked again.

"The key is to outsmart them," Francis told the girls. "And I think I know how." Then he told them his plan.

On the day of the parade, Francis was finally able to get out of bed. After wishing the Blueberries good luck, he went to join the other circus bugs to wait for the parade to begin. Everyone was very excited about it.

The Boysenberries had put berry juice along the parade path so the Blueberries would slip in it. The boys hid nearby waiting for them to pass.

Suddenly, the Boysenberries heard the sounds of the parade. But it wasn't anywhere near them!

"Hey!" cried one of the boys. "What's going on?"

The Boysenberries ran out into the road. They slipped and slid in their own berry juice! They had been tricked! The Blueberries had chosen another route.

"Look at that flag!" Francis said to his friends as the Blueberries approached. "Isn't it great?"

The troop stopped in front of Francis and saluted.

"Well done, girls," Francis said.

The Blueberries cheered. Francis smiled and shook his head.

Those little Blueberries sure had grown on him. Maybe being a den mother isn't so bad, after all! he thought.

Disney's

The Fox and the Hound

Friends–No Matter What!

One day, an old woman named Widow Tweed discovered an orphaned fox in her farmyard. She tried to pick him up by the scruff of his neck, but he was nimble and quick.

"Oh, my, my!" she cried. "You're a feisty little rascal, aren't you?"

Widow Tweed decided that she couldn't just leave the baby fox all by himself, so she took him into her house and fed him from a bottle.

"You're such a little toddler," she marveled. "Say, that's what I'm going to call you . . . Tod."

So Tod happily became part of Widow Tweed's life, and she was glad to have someone to keep her company.

Unfortunately, the fox had a habit of getting into mischief, for he was very curious and loved exploring the farm. One afternoon, he chased a butterfly right onto Amos Slade's property. Amos was a hard-nosed man with one thing on his mind: hunting. Even his trusty dog, Chief, had been trained for it.

Amos had just brought home a new puppy named Copper. It was Chief's duty to look after the pup.

Copper smelled something peculiar in the yard. He wondered what it could be.

"Hey there, Copper," said Chief. "What are you sniffing at?"

"Something I never smelled before, Chief," replied the pup. But he was determined to find out what the smell was.

"The master isn't going to like you wandering off," warned Chief.

"I won't get lost," Copper reassured him. "I can smell my way back!"

The puppy went into a hollow log.

"What are you smelling?" a voice asked. It was Tod, peering down at Copper from atop the log.

The dog sniffed at Tod and realized he'd found the smell he'd been looking for.

Tod introduced himself and explained that he was a fox.

"I'm a hound dog," said Copper.

The two played hide-and-seek. Copper followed his nose to find Tod wherever the fox hid. They had so much fun, they met the next day and played some more.

"Copper, you're my very best friend," Tod said as he tackled the dog a few days later.

"And you're mine, too, Tod," Copper replied, smiling.

"And we'll always be friends forever, won't we?" asked Tod.

"Yeah," agreed Copper, "forever."

However, Amos Slade had other plans for Copper. Plans that involved hunting. Amos was furious that the pup kept wandering off. He wanted a dog that would obey him.

So when Copper returned, Amos tied the hound to his doghouse.

The next day, Tod waited for Copper, but he never showed up. The fox went looking for his friend.

"Hey, Copper, why didn't you . . . Golly, you're all tied up!" Tod exclaimed. He felt terrible.

"We can play around here," Tod suggested.

102

Curiously, the fox walked up to Chief, who was sleeping in his barrel.

"Oh, don't go in there!" Copper warned quietly. "He can get awful cranky."

"Gee, is he ever big!" Tod exclaimed.

Sniff, sniff. Even in his sleep, Chief knew the scent of a fox.

"Grr . . . ruff!" barked Chief. He was awake!

Frightened, Tod started to run away. Amos came out with his rifle and fired. *Bang! Bang!*

Luckily, Widow Tweed was driving by. Tod jumped on the back of her truck.

Amos was mad as thunder. He went to Widow Tweed's house. "If I ever catch that fox on my property again, I'll blast him!" he yelled. "And next time, I won't miss!"

The next day, Amos took the dogs away for a long hunting trip. Tod watched as they drove off. All winter, he missed his friend. Big Mama the owl told him things would be different after hunting season. She explained that dogs and foxes were meant to be enemies. But Tod was positive it would make no difference that he was a fox. Copper was his best friend—no matter what.

The night Copper returned, Tod crept quietly over to visit his old friend. They had both grown a lot and looked quite different.

"It's good to see you, Tod, but you shouldn't be here," warned Copper. "You're going to get us both into a lot of trouble."

"Look, I just wanted to see you," the fox explained. "We're still friends, aren't we?"

"Those days are over," said Copper. "I'm a hunting dog now."

Tod couldn't believe what he was hearing! How could his friend have forgotten all the great times they had shared?

Sadly, Tod turned to leave. But Chief had woken up and was barking loudly. Amos ran onto the porch with his rifle. "It's that fox again! After him, boys!" yelled the hunter.

Tod ran for his life as Copper and Chief chased him. When Copper finally cornered the fox, he suddenly had second thoughts. "Tod, I don't want to see you get killed," he said. "I'll let you go this one time." True to his word, when Amos caught up to Copper, the hound led the hunter in the wrong direction.

Tod was relieved and overjoyed. Copper still cared about him!

Unfortunately, Chief did not. The big dog caught sight of the fox. He chased him onto a bridge, but a train was coming. They were trapped!

Thinking quickly, Tod lay between the rails. The train passed over him. But Chief was too slow. The train hit him, and he fell into the river below.

Copper raced toward Chief. The dog was lying on the rocks, hurt but alive.

"Chief? Chief!" called Copper. "Oh, no!" It's my fault, he thought as he helped the injured dog. Chief was like a father to him. Copper felt guilty and angry, but most of all he blamed Tod. As Amos planned revenge, Copper joined him.

Copper looked up at the fox on the tracks and growled. "Tod, if it's the last thing I do, I'll get you for this!" he vowed.

Everything had changed. That night, the fox and the hound went their separate ways.

Widow Tweed decided that the safest place for Tod would be a game preserve, where there was no hunting. She would miss Tod terribly, but at least he'd be far from Amos Slade and his rifle.

Tod didn't like the forest preserve. It was big and scary and he was lonely. Luckily, Big Mama the owl knew another fox who lived there. She was named Vixey. Tod had never seen anyone so beautiful!

"I just know you're going to love the forest," Vixey told him. "Let me show you around."

Tod agreed, thrilled to have made a new friend.

In another area of the game preserve, Amos, with Copper by his side, stared at a sign that read NO HUNTING. But that didn't stop him for a second.

As soon as Copper picked up Tod's scent, Amos set out some traps. Before long, Tod stepped in one, barely missing its snapping jaws. Tod and Vixey ran away quickly. Panting, Tod looked behind him and saw Amos and Copper face-to-face with a giant bear! Tod watched as the hound tried to protect Amos by jumping on the bear and grabbing his neck with his teeth. But the bear swatted Copper with his huge paw.

Tod couldn't abandon his old friend. He jumped on the bear's back, biting his ears. The bear roared with pain, threw the fox off, and then followed Tod onto a log bridge. But the bear's weight caused the log to break, and Tod and the bear tumbled down toward a waterfall below.

Weak and breathless, Tod looked up to see Amos pointing a rifle at him.

"Tod?" Copper called out to his old friend.

The fox barely looked up.

Then Copper bravely stood over Tod. The dog's eyes pleaded with Amos. Finally, the hunter lowered his rifle.

"Oh, well, c'mon boy," said Amos. "Let's go home."

Before he left, Copper turned back to look at Tod one last time. They knew they'd always be friends—no matter what.

Disney's
The Rescuers

A FRIEND IN NEED

The mice of the Rescue Aid Society were holding a special meeting at their headquarters in New York. Some of the members had found a note asking for help from a little girl named Penny.

"Oh, that poor little girl!" cried Miss Bianca. "Mr. Chairman, please may I have this assignment?" The society often sent its mice on rescue missions.

The chairman was reluctant to let the elegant mouse go by herself, so Miss Bianca chose a co-agent: Mr. Bernard, the janitor! But he wasn't sure he wanted to go.

"We'll be a great team!" Miss Bianca insisted. She was so charming that Bernard agreed.

That night, the pair set off for the orphanage named in Penny's note.

When they arrived at the orphanage, the mice climbed through a window and began to look around for clues. Soon, they noticed a cat peering down at them!

The mice panicked, but the cat was old and friendly. His name was Rufus, and he loved Penny. He told them how she had been sad lately because no one wanted to adopt her. The cat had reassured her that one day she would have parents of her own.

"But the next thing I heard, Penny was gone," Rufus continued. He explained that no one knew where she was, and that even the police had given up looking.

Then the cat remembered something: a lady who ran a pawnshop had tried to give Penny a ride in her car.

As the mice left to investigate, Rufus wondered how they would be able to help Penny—they were so small, after all.

Moments later, Bernard and Bianca slipped inside Medusa's Pawnshop and spotted a schoolbook lying on a counter. They looked inside and saw Penny's name!

"Then she's gotta be here," Bernard said.

Before they could search for her, the phone rang. The mice scrambled into hiding as Medusa stormed into the room. "You blundering fool!" she snarled into the phone. "Can't you control a little girl? I'm taking the next flight down to Devil's Bayou."

Medusa hurled clothes—and without realizing it, Bernard—into a suitcase! Bianca grabbed onto a strap that was hanging from the suitcase as Medusa left.

Soon, they were all in a car headed for the airport. Bianca scurried over to the suitcase, opened it, and hopped in. But Medusa drove like a madwoman. When she made a fast turn, the suitcase bounced out of the car, taking the two mice with it.

Bernard and Bianca walked the rest of the way to the airport, then headed for the Albatross Airlines terminal. As they sat in the ramshackle office, they watched as their pilot, Captain Orville, came in for a crash-landing.

"Maybe we'd better take the train," suggested Bernard nervously.

But Bianca couldn't wait to be soaring above the clouds on the albatross's back. When Orville was ready, they boarded and took off.

They flew over the city and then down the coastline toward bayou country. From what Medusa had said on the phone, Bernard and Bianca felt sure they would find Penny down there.

Day turned to night, and Bernard's jumpiness finally turned to contentment as Bianca put her head on his shoulder and fell fast asleep.

A F R I E N D   I N   N E E D

In the bayou, Medusa and her partner, Snoops, were searching the swamp for Penny, who had run away. A giant diamond called the Devil's Eye was hidden in a nearby cave, and Medusa wasn't small enough to fit inside and search for it. That's why she'd kidnapped Penny—and why she had to find her.

The villains shot a flare to light up the night—and hit Orville as he flew by. "My rudder's on fire! Bail out!" yelled the albatross.

Bernard and Bianca used their umbrella as a parachute, and Orville steered himself toward the water. Luckily, the three travelers landed safely outside the house of Orville's friends, Ellie Mae and Luke. The swamp creatures immediately summoned Evinrude the dragonfly to help rescue Penny. The tiny creature had the fastest leaf boat on the bayou. Bernard and Bianca stepped into the tiny craft, and within minutes, the speedy insect was motoring them across the swamp.

Meanwhile, Medusa's pet crocodiles, Brutus and Nero, had found Penny and brought her back to the criminals' riverboat hideout.

"You'd better behave, or I'll let Nero and Brutus have your old teddy bear," threatened Snoops.

Bernard and Bianca arrived just in time to hear Medusa tell Snoops she was going to send Penny down into the cave again.

Before the pair could reach Penny, the crocodiles began to chase them, and soon Snoops and Medusa were after the mice, too. They summoned Evinrude and were able to get back to the swamp safely. There, they wondered what to do next.

"Maybe Rufus was right," said Bernard. "What can two little mice do?"

"But Bernard, the society is counting on us!" Bianca declared. "We can't quit now!"

Later that night, the determined mice returned to the hideout and located Penny. They told her they'd found the message she'd sent and come to rescue her.

"Didn't you bring somebody big with you?" Penny asked.

"The three of us need to work together and have a little faith," said Bianca.

"Rufus said faith makes things turn out right," Penny agreed.

Penny and the mice sent Evinrude to get help from Ellie Mae and the other swamp critters. Then, when Medusa came to take Penny back to the cave, the mice hid inside the little girl's pocket. No matter what happened next, Penny would not be alone. Bernard and Bianca would be with her every step of the way.

Medusa and Snoops lowered Penny through the cave's small opening. "You get down there and find that big diamond or you will never see that teddy again!" the evil woman exclaimed.

Once they were inside the cave, Bernard and Bianca popped out of Penny's pocket to help her search for the gem.

They found it inside a skull, but it was wedged too tightly for Penny to move. As she struggled to free the diamond, the little girl noticed that the water inside the cave was starting to rise.

"Please pull me up!" Penny called to Medusa.

"Not until you get the diamond!" Medusa threatened.

Bianca and Bernard knew their only hope was to use teamwork. The girl pried the jewel loose while the two mice pushed it out of the skull. They had the diamond!

Just then, water gushed into the
cave and Bernard and Bianca
got caught in a whirlpool.

Penny swam to her friends.
Once she had placed them
safely in a bucket, she climbed in, too.

"I've got the diamond!" the girl yelled to Snoops and Medusa.
The villains hoisted them up.

"The Devil's Eye!" Medusa cried joyfully. "It's mine, all mine."

A few minutes later, Penny asked Medusa to return her teddy
bear. But Medusa clutched the bear tightly. "Teddy goes with me,
dear," she informed Penny as she backed through the doorway.

Luckily, Bernard and Bianca had already sprung into action.
They tripped Medusa, and the teddy bear flew into the air. When
Penny rescued him, she discovered that Medusa had hidden the
diamond inside him for safekeeping!

All at once, Evinrude and the other swamp creatures appeared. They trapped the crocodiles, smacked Medusa on the head with a rolling pin, and ignited some fireworks. While Medusa and Snoops dodged rockets, Penny jumped into the villains' swampmobile. The boat wouldn't start, but Ellie Mae found some fuel and filled the tank. Penny sped away—Bernard, Bianca, teddy bear, and all.

Medusa wasn't going to let her diamond get away that easily, though! She jumped from her sinking riverboat and grabbed onto a rope that was hanging from the back of the swampmobile. The evil woman felt certain victory was hers—until the rope broke and launched her into the riverboat's smokestack.

"We did it!" cried Bernard and Bianca. "Hooray!"

"There goes my diamond!" Medusa wailed. But that was the least of her problems—crocodiles were snapping at her from the water below!

A few days later, the mice of the Rescue Aid Society gathered in front of a television to watch Penny on the news. The diamond had been given to a museum, and Penny had been adopted!

"I didn't do it all by myself," Penny announced. "Two little mice from the Rescue Aid Society helped me."

Bernard and Bianca were overjoyed. Their friend was safe and happy.

Moments later, Evinrude arrived with a note from a stranger asking for help.

"Come on," said Bianca to Bernard. "Let's go!" They knew another new friend was just a rescue mission away!

DISNEY'S
THE JUNGLE BOOK

Mowgli Finds a Friend

One day, deep in the jungles of India, a strange sound echoed through the trees. Bagheera the panther heard the noise and ran along the riverbank. He followed it until he found a boat that had landed on the shore. Inside, a baby boy was crying. When the baby saw the panther, he smiled. Bagheera decided to take the boy to a wolf family that lived nearby. The mother had just had a litter of pups, and Bagheera thought she might be able to look after one more baby.

When the mother wolf saw the boy, she agreed to take care of him. She named him Mowgli, and for ten years she raised him as one of her own. Mowgli was a very happy Man-cub. He spent his days running and playing with his wolf brothers and sisters. One day, bad news arrived in the jungle.

Shere Khan the tiger had returned after a long absence. The tiger was mean and hated everything. But more than anything, he hated Man.

That meant it was no longer safe for Mowgli to live in the jungle. The wolves decided that he should go to a Man-village at once.

Bagheera had kept watch over Mowgli through the years and volunteered to take him. The wolves accepted his offer. Later that night, the boy rode on the panther's back as they made their way through the jungle. Mowgli soon grew tired. "Shouldn't we start back home?" he asked sleepily.

Bagheera shook his head. "We're not going back," the panther said. "I'm taking you to the Man-village."

But Mowgli did not want to leave the jungle. It was his home. "I don't want to go to the Man-village!" he shouted. Then he added, "I can take care of myself."

"You wouldn't last one day," Bagheera said. Then he led Mowgli up a tree where they would sleep for the night.

The next morning, Bagheera was ready to continue to the village. Mowgli grabbed on to a nearby tree trunk. "I'm staying right here," he declared. The panther tried to pull him away, but Mowgli held on tight. Finally, Bagheera pulled so hard that he lost his grip and went flying into a large pond.

"That does it!" cried the panther. "From now on, you're on your own." Then Bagheera walked into the jungle brush and disappeared.

Mowgli headed in the opposite direction. "I can take care of myself," he said aloud. A little later, he sat down in the shade. As he rested, he began to worry that maybe he *couldn't* take care of himself.

Just then, a bear named Baloo walked out of the jungle and spotted him. A Man-cub in the jungle was an unusual sight, so the friendly bear walked over to sniff him. Mowgli reached out and slapped Baloo right on the nose.

"Ouch!" the bear cried. "I'm just trying to be friendly!"

"Go away and leave me alone," Mowgli said with a scowl.

But Baloo did not listen. He sat down next to the Man-cub and patted him on the back. "That's pretty big talk, Little Britches," the bear said. Then he decided that Mowgli needed to have some fun. Baloo jumped up and started bobbing and weaving like a boxer. "Hey, kid, Baloo's gonna learn you to fight like a bear."

The bear's silly behavior made Mowgli laugh, and soon he was dancing around and boxing just like Baloo. When they finished, Mowgli jumped up on his new friend's stomach and tickled him. "You're all right, kid," Baloo said gently.

Just then, Bagheera walked over to them. He had returned to make sure Mowgli was okay. The panther told Baloo that he thought Mowgli should go to the Man-village so he'd be safe from Shere Khan.

Baloo didn't want his little buddy to go to a Man-village. "They'll ruin him. They'll make a man out of him," the bear said.

Bagheera sighed. He knew Mowgli would never leave now that he had made friends with Baloo. The panther watched as the pair jumped into the river and floated lazily away.

Suddenly, a group of monkeys grabbed Mowgli! They began to toss him back and forth. "Give me back my Man-cub!" shouted Baloo. But the monkeys ignored the bear and carried Mowgli away. Baloo found Bagheera, and the two followed the monkeys deep into the jungle.

The monkeys took Mowgli to their leader, King Louie, who lived amid ancient ruins. The monkey king wanted to make a deal. If the Man-cub taught him how to make fire, then Louie would help him stay in the jungle.

"But I don't know how to make fire," said Mowgli.

King Louie didn't believe him. He danced around, trying to convince the Man-cub to tell him the secret of Man's fire.

When Bagheera and Baloo arrived at the ruins, they saw Mowgli dancing with the monkeys. Bagheera told Baloo to distract the king. The bear knew exactly what to do. He dressed up like a big female monkey, and batted his eyelashes at King Louie.

Just as Bagheera was about to rescue Mowgli, Baloo's disguise fell off. The monkeys chased the three friends all over the ruins. Then Louie ran into a column, and the ruins began to fall down. Mowgli, Baloo, and Bagheera hurried away.

Later, as Mowgli lay sleeping, Bagheera tried to make Baloo see that the Man-cub wasn't safe in the jungle—especially with Shere Khan around. Baloo knew the panther was right.

The next morning, Baloo and the Man-cub began walking. "Where are we going?" Mowgli asked after a while.

Baloo gulped. "Ah, look, little buddy . . . I need to take you to the Man-village. It's where you belong," he stammered.

"But you said we were partners!" Mowgli yelled. "You said I could stay with you!" The Man-cub raced away. Sadly, he sat down on a log as a light rain began to fall. All of a sudden, Shere Khan appeared! "You don't scare me," Mowgli said. He picked up a heavy branch and prepared to fight the tiger.

Shere Khan snarled and lunged at Mowgli.

Just as Shere Khan was about to land on the Man-cub, he crashed to the ground. Baloo had arrived and grabbed on to the tiger's tail! "Run, Mowgli, run!" the bear cried.

While Baloo struggled to keep the tiger away from Mowgli, lightning struck nearby, causing a fire. The Man-cub picked up a burning branch and tied it to Shere Khan's tail.

When the mighty tiger saw the fire, he let out a terrified roar and ran for his life.

Mowgli had defeated Shere Khan! But not everyone had escaped unharmed. Baloo was lying on the ground . . . and he wasn't moving.

"Baloo, get up," Mowgli begged. But Baloo didn't respond.

Bagheera walked into the clearing. Seeing the bear lying on the ground, he started to comfort Mowgli.

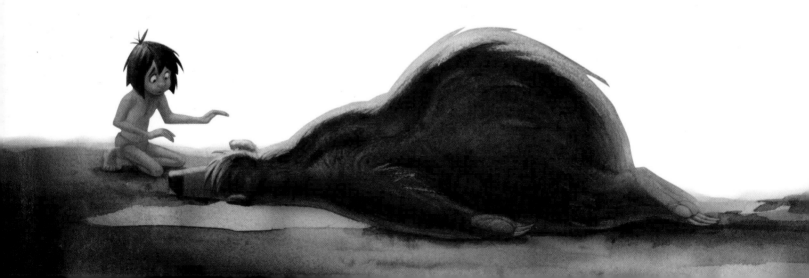

Suddenly, the panther was interrupted by a familiar voice. "I'm all right, Little Britches!" cried Baloo. "I was just taking five, you know, playing it cool."

"Baloo, you're alive!" Mowgli exclaimed, throwing his arms around his friend.

After Baloo got up, the three friends left the clearing and made their way back into the jungle. Suddenly, Mowgli heard someone singing. "I want to take a closer look," he told Baloo and Bagheera. Climbing up a tree, he saw a girl. When she noticed him, she giggled. Mowgli turned to his friends and shrugged his shoulders.

Baloo and Bagheera watched as he began to follow her into the Man-village. "Mowgli, come back!" Baloo cried.

"Let him go," said Bagheera.

Baloo sighed. He knew it was the right thing to do. His little buddy had a new home. "I still think he would have made a great bear," Baloo said. Then, he put his arm around Bagheera and the two headed back into the jungle—happy that their friend was going to the place where he belonged.

DISNEP'S
THE
LION KING

A Lion's Best Friends

Mufasa, the lion king, was the ruler of the Pride Lands. When his son, Simba, was born, the animals bowed in respect as the wise baboon, Rafiki, presented the cub. They knew that someday Simba would be their leader. It was all part of the Circle of Life.

Until Simba was born, his uncle Scar had been next in line to be king. There was nothing that the greedy lion wanted more. So he devised an evil plan.

"Your father has a surprise for you," Scar told his nephew one morning as he led him into a deep gorge. "Just stay on this rock, and I'll go get him."

Eager for his surprise, the cub obeyed. He didn't know that Scar had instructed some hyenas to scare a herd of wildebeests into a stampede— straight toward him. Nor did the cub know that Scar had run off to warn Mufasa that his only son was in danger.

It was a trap—and it worked!

Just as Scar had hoped, Mufasa leaped into the gorge and raced toward Simba, who was dangling from a branch. By the time the lion king carried Simba to the safety of a rocky ledge, he had become very tired.

For a moment, the stampeding wildebeests almost carried Mufasa away. But he clung to the rocky gorge wall and slowly began to claw his way up the side.

"Brother, help me!" Mufasa cried to Scar.

Instead of helping, though, Scar dug his claws into his brother's paws. He smiled wickedly as Mufasa fell to his death.

Unfortunately for Scar, Simba was still alive. But the evil lion knew just how to get rid of him.

"If it weren't for you, your father would still be alive," he told the cub, who hadn't seen what Scar had done. "Run away . . . and never return!"

And that is just what Simba did.

Simba ran until the ground grew hard and cracked beneath his blistered paws and his small, sore legs collapsed from exhaustion.

He fell asleep at once. But when he woke up, things were very different.

The desert had turned into a lush jungle. And instead of being

alone, he was with a warthog named Pumbaa and a meerkat named Timon.

"We saved you!" cried the meerkat.

Timon and Pumbaa could tell that something was bothering Simba. But the cub didn't want to talk about it—and that was just fine with them.

Their motto, after all, was *hakuna matata,* which meant *no worries!*

"You got to put your past behind you," Timon told Simba.

Timon and Pumbaa didn't care a bit what the cub thought he had done.

They liked him and wanted him to stay in the jungle. So he did.

Of course, Simba had to get used to a few things, such as having no zebras or antelopes or hippos to eat. Instead, Timon introduced him to a new kind of food: grubs! The cub also ate termites, ladybugs, and all the other insects that crawled around the jungle.

"You'll learn to love them!" Pumbaa told him.

Simba didn't think he ever would, but he ate them anyway.

What the lion cub *did* love were his
new friends.

With Timon and Pumbaa,
every day brought new
games and fun-filled
adventures. When
they weren't playing,
they were eating;
when they weren't
eating, they were
playing; and when
they weren't doing either,
they just relaxed.

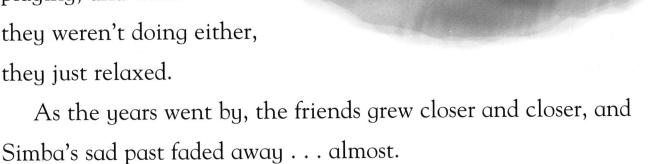

As the years went by, the friends grew closer and closer, and
Simba's sad past faded away . . . almost.

One day, while Timon and Pumbaa were out stalking beetles, a stranger appeared in the jungle: a fierce lioness, alone and very hungry!

"*Aaaaggh!*" yelled Pumbaa, as he fled. But the warthog got stuck beneath an old tree root.

"*Aaaaggh!*" screamed Timon, as he tried to push Pumbaa to freedom before the lioness attacked them.

Luckily, Simba heard his friends' cries and raced to their defense. Now fully grown, he easily wrestled the lioness to the ground—but she quickly flipped him over and pinned *him* down. Only then did he realize whom he was fighting.

"Nala?" he said. She was one of his old playmates!

Nala was surprised to see him. Scar had told the whole pride that Simba was dead! She told her old friend that Scar had let the hyenas take over the Pride Lands. "Everything's destroyed. There's no food or water. You're our only hope!" she cried.

When Timon, Pumbaa, and Nala woke up the next morning, Simba was gone.

"The king has returned," Rafiki informed them.

At first, Timon and Pumbaa didn't understand. But Nala did. She told them about Scar and how he had taken over as king and ruined the once great Pride Lands.

"Simba must fight his uncle to take his place as king," she explained. She also told them that he might need a little help.

"If it's important to Simba," Timon said, "we're with him to the end."

156

Timon, Pumbaa, and Nala hurried to catch up with Simba. They followed him to the Pride Lands.

Once there, Simba let out an earthshaking roar and climbed Pride Rock to face his evil uncle.

"Step down, Scar," Simba commanded.

But his uncle wasn't going to give up the kingdom so easily. Scar and the hyenas fought, and soon Simba was dangling from a cliff.

"This is just the way your father looked before he died," sneered Scar.

Suddenly, Simba realized that *Scar* was the one responsible for Mufasa's death—not him! Filled with rage, he sprang onto the ledge. With Timon, Pumbaa, and Nala beside him, he took on Scar and the hyenas.

The friends fought bravely. Scar attacked Simba, but the younger lion quickly moved out of the way. Scar fell to his death. The hyenas soon retreated. The battle over, Simba immediately became king.

Under Simba's wise and just rule, the Pride Lands soon returned to their former splendor. Simba went on to become as great a king as his father. He and Nala soon had a cub of their own.

The Circle of Life continued, as it was always meant to. Simba lived happily ever after . . . along with two better and truer friends than any lion king ever had!

Nemo and
the Ghost Fish

"Have a great day, Nemo!" Marlin said as he hugged his son good-bye. He and Dory were dropping Nemo off at school. "Are you feeling ready to learn?"

"I'm feeling it!" Nemo replied enthusiastically.

"That's what I like to hear," said Marlin. "Now go on and expand your mind. Beef up the brain! Flex your mental muscle!"

"All right!" Nemo exclaimed. "I will . . . just as soon as you let go."

Marlin realized he was still hugging his son. "Oh, right!" Marlin said with a chuckle. With one final squeeze, he let go.

Nemo went to join his classmates and his teacher, Mr. Ray. "Bye, Dad!" the little clown fish called out. "Bye, Dory! See you after school!"

Nemo loved school. So did his friends, Tad, Pearl, and Sheldon. How could they not when Mr. Ray made everything so much fun? He took the class exploring all over the reef. Every day, Nemo and his classmates got an up-close look at all kinds of sea life.

Today, Mr. Ray took them to a clearing on the ocean floor. "Okay, explorers," he said, "now it's time to do a little exploring on your own. Let's see if each of you can find a shell. Then we'll identify them together!"

The youngsters fanned out. Nemo searched in the shadow of some coral. Pearl peeked into algae. Sheldon dug in the sand.

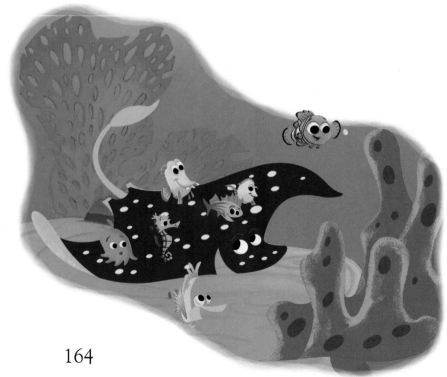

Tad was the first of Nemo's friends to find something. "Hey, guys!" he cried. "Look at this!"

Nemo, Pearl, and Sheldon swam over to the butterfly fish. They crowded around Tad and stared in wonder at the gleaming white shell he held in his fin.

"Cooooool," said Sheldon.

"It's heart-shaped!" Nemo exclaimed.

"It's so pretty," said Pearl. "Where did you find it?"

Tad pointed to a cave. "In there," he said. "I'll show you. Maybe there are more!" Tad darted toward the cave entrance.

"Yeah!" said Pearl, following him. "I want to find one, too."

"Me, too!" cried Sheldon, swimming after them. "Are you coming, Nemo?" he called.

"Nah," Nemo replied. "You guys go on." He wanted to find a shell that was different from everybody else's.

Only a few minutes had passed before Nemo heard an odd noise. He looked up and saw Tad, Pearl, and Sheldon bolting out of the cave at full speed, screaming very loudly.

"What's the matter?" Nemo asked. "Is it a barracuda? An eel?"

Sheldon shook his head. "No, worse!" he replied. He was shaking and his eyes were wide with fear. "It's a *g-g-ghost fish*!"

"Yeah, right," Nemo replied. Then he noticed Tad's fin was empty. "Where's your shell?" he asked.

Tad looked down. "Aw, shucks," he said, his voice heavy with disappointment. "I was going to give it to my mom." Then he peered into the cave. "I must have dropped it in there. But I'm not going back for it. No way! Not with that ghost fish on the loose!"

Nemo looked at the dark cave opening. "Don't worry," he told Tad. "I'll find your shell."

Without looking back, the little clown fish swam bravely into the cave.

"See?" he said to himself. "Nothing to be afraid of. Just a dark underwater cave." Nemo ventured deeper into the cave, scanning the sandy bottom for Tad's shell.

Then, he froze. On the cave wall next to him was a huge, fish-shaped shadow.

Nemo took a deep breath. "Stay calm and be polite," he whispered to himself. "Uh, excuse me, Mr. Ghost Fish? Or is it Ms. Ghost Fish?"

"A ghost fish?!" a tiny voice said nervously. "Where? Where? Don't let it get me!"

The ghost fish didn't *sound* very scary. Nemo swam closer to the shadow. "Are *you* afraid of ghost fish?" he asked it.

"Yeah!" squeaked the little voice. "Who isn't?"

This time, the voice didn't seem to be coming from the shadow. Nemo swam to his left. There, cowering behind a rock, was a little fish, glowing softly with a pale orange light.

Nemo smiled and breathed a sigh of relief. The ghost fish wasn't a ghost fish at all. It was just a spooky-looking shadow that had been caused by the glow-in-the-dark fish's light shining on an oddly shaped piece of coral.

Nemo's fear was forgotten. "Oh, hi!" he called out to the glowing fish.

Startled, the little fish darted behind another rock. Then, timidly, he peeked out from behind it to study Nemo.

"Don't be afraid," Nemo said. "I'm just a little fish— like you." He smiled and reached out his fin, inviting the glowing fish to come out into the open. "My name's Nemo. What's yours?"

The fish swam out cautiously. "Eddy," he replied, his eyes still wide. "You mean there's no ghost fish?"

Nemo chuckled. "I thought *you* were the ghost fish!" He explained the whole funny story to Eddy.

"By the way," said Nemo, "how do you glow like that?"

Eddy shrugged. "I just do," he replied. "My whole family does."

Nemo thought he knew someone who would know more about Eddy's glow: Mr. Ray! So Nemo invited Eddy to meet his teacher and his friends. Then, swimming together out of the cave, they laughed over the way they had met.

"You really thought *I* was a ghost fish?" Eddy said with a giggle.

Outside, Nemo apologized to Tad. "Sorry I didn't find your shell," Nemo said. "But I did find your ghost fish!"

Then Nemo and Eddy told their tale. Before long, the ghost fish was forgotten. Instead, everyone wanted to know more about Eddy.

"Can you glow different colors?" Pearl asked.

"If I touch you, will I get burned?" Sheldon wanted to know.

"How come the water doesn't put out your light?" asked Tad. Nemo wanted to know what made Eddy glow.

"Good question, Nemo," Mr. Ray replied. "See these patches on either side of Eddy's jaw? Inside them are teeny-tiny glow-in-the-dark organisms. When you see Eddy glow, you're really seeing those organisms glowing."

Everyone ooohed and aaahed over Eddy's glow patches.

"If you think that's cool," said Eddy, "you should come meet the rest of my family!"

Eddy led the whole class into the cave to show them his glow-in-the-dark world—including his family. Nemo thought it was one of the most beautiful things he had ever seen, but there was still one thing weighing on his mind.

"Mr. Ray," Nemo whispered to his teacher, "I didn't finish the assignment. I mean, I didn't find a shell."

Mr. Ray laughed. "That's okay, Nemo," he replied. "I'd say you still get an A in Exploring for today!"

WALT DISNEY'S

Lady and the TRAMP

Unlikely Friends

Lady, a beautiful cocker spaniel, loved her owners. On the day she came home, she overheard them talking to each other and realized their names must be Jim Dear and Darling. Every morning, Lady woke Jim Dear for work. She brought him his slippers and fetched the newspaper. During the day she kept Darling company, and they always enjoyed an afternoon walk together.

When Lady was six months old, she received her first collar and license. After Darling put it on her, Lady happily pranced outside. She was excited to show her best friends, Jock the Scottish terrier and Trusty the bloodhound.

They admired her license. Lady held her head high. She was so proud!

On the other side of town, Tramp was a mutt who wasn't what most people would have called respectable. He didn't have owners or a home of his own. He was footloose and collar-free, but he was also very clever. He had a good heart and often rescued his friends from the clutches of the dogcatcher. He didn't want them to have to go to the pound.

Tramp loved going on chases. One afternoon, he tricked and teased the dogcatcher until he'd lost him. Then he looked around and noticed he was in a ritzy part of town.

"Snob Hill," he muttered. He was glad he didn't live in this kind of neighborhood. It looked boring. "Wonder what the leash-and-collar set does for excitement."

Curious, Tramp wandered into a yard and overheard Lady and her friends. "It's something I've done, I guess," Lady was saying sadly. "Jim Dear and Darling are acting so strangely."

Jock and Trusty simply smiled. They knew what the problem was. Darling was expecting a baby!

Lady was confused. "What's a baby?" she asked.

"Just a cute little bundle of trouble," Tramp piped up.

Lady looked bewildered. She'd never seen this strange dog before. He didn't even have a collar on!

Tramp continued. "Remember those nice juicy cuts of beef? Forget 'em. And that nice warm bed by the fire? How about a leaky doghouse instead?"

Jock told Lady not to listen to the dog. Then he turned to Tramp and told him to leave.

"Okay, okay," Tramp replied. Before he left, he warned Lady, "Remember, when a baby moves in, the dog moves out!"

Lady was worried, but luckily Tramp's predictions did not come true. When the baby was born, Darling showed her to Lady, who loved the child instantly!

Every day, Lady watched over the baby. Jim Dear and Darling petted her proudly. When they decided to take a short vacation, they knew the baby would be in good hands. Besides, Darling's aunt, Sarah, would be there to help.

But Aunt Sarah wouldn't let Lady near the baby. Even worse, she had brought two sneaky Siamese cats with her. When Aunt Sarah was out of the room, the cats tried to eat the goldfish. Then they ripped the curtains. Lady tried to stop the cats, but her barking angered Aunt Sarah.

"Oh! Merciful heavens!" Aunt Sarah cried when she came downstairs. The cats had made it look like Lady had messed up the room and attacked *them*.

Aunt Sarah was furious. She dragged Lady to the pet store to fit her with a muzzle! Lady was upset—she hadn't done anything wrong. As soon as the salesman put the muzzle on her, Lady ran out of the store. Cars screeched by. Tin cans got caught on her leash and made a horrendous racket. Then ferocious dogs chased her. Lady was terrified.

Suddenly, Tramp appeared! He fought the bullies and rescued Lady.

"What are you doing on this side of the tracks?" he asked. Just then he noticed the muzzle. "Aw, you poor kid. We've got to get this thing off. Come on!" he said.

Tramp led Lady through town to the zoo. There, they found a beaver building a dam. The beaver easily bit through the muzzle strap and freed Lady!

Lady felt grateful—both to the beaver and to Tramp.

Tramp wanted to show Lady how great life could be for a dog who wasn't part of a family. He decided to take her to a special Italian restaurant. Tony, the owner, loved Tramp.

"Where you been-a so long?" Tony asked. "What's this-a? Hey, Joe, look—he's gotta new girlfriend."

Lady blushed.

"Tonight-a he's getting best in the house!" Tony said to Joe, who worked at the restaurant.

"Okay, Tony," said Joe. "You're da boss."

Tramp and Lady looked at the menu. Then Tramp barked.

Tony knew exactly what Tramp wanted and before long, he returned with a huge platter of spaghetti and meatballs. Then he and Joe serenaded the dogs.

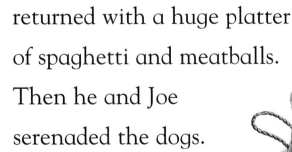

Without meaning to, the dogs began to eat the same piece of spaghetti. They didn't realize what had happened until their lips met in a kiss. Then Tramp rolled the last meatball toward Lady. She was touched by his generosity. He was different from what she'd thought. He felt the same way about her. As they stared into each other's eyes, it was clear that they had fallen in love.

It was a beautiful night. Lady and Tramp walked side by side through empty streets. The sky was lit with stars, and the moon was full. They went to a grassy hill in the park and fell asleep.

The next morning Lady was worried. "I should have been home hours ago!" she cried. Unlike Tramp, she liked belonging to a family.

But Tramp wanted to chase chickens to show Lady how much fun his life was. Unfortunately, a dogcatcher appeared and threw Lady in his wagon.

When Aunt Sarah picked Lady up from the pound, she was so angry that she chained her to the doghouse. Lady was heartbroken. Now she wouldn't be able to see the baby.

That evening, Lady saw a rat climb through the window of the baby's room! She barked wildly, trying to warn Aunt Sarah.

But the old woman simply opened the window and yelled at her. "Hush now! Stop that racket!"

Luckily, Tramp was nearby and heard Lady's cries. "What's wrong?" he asked.

"A rat! Upstairs in the baby's room!" Lady cried.

Bravely, Tramp raced into the house through the doggie door. Lady finally broke free from her chain and followed him up to the baby's room. Tramp fought the rat—and won. Although the two knocked over everything in sight, the baby was safe. Lady was so proud of Tramp.

But Aunt Sarah did not see the rat. She only saw that the crib had been knocked over. She locked Lady in the cellar and shoved Tramp into a closet. Then she called to have the dogcatcher take Tramp away.

Jim Dear and Darling arrived home just as the dogcatcher was putting Tramp in his wagon.

"What's going on here?" asked Jim Dear.

"Just picking up a stray, mister," said the dogcatcher. "Caught him attacking a baby."

Jim Dear and Darling looked at each other worriedly and rushed inside. "Aunt Sarah? Aunt Sarah!" they called.

The old woman tried to explain what had happened. Against her wishes, Jim Dear and Darling let Lady out of the cellar. The cocker spaniel quickly ran upstairs, barking.

"Keep her away!" Aunt Sarah cried.

"Nonsense," said Jim Dear. "She's trying to tell us something. What is it, old girl?"

Lady led him to the baby's room and uncovered the dead rat. Jim Dear realized what had happened. Tramp was a hero! Jim Dear and Lady went to rescue him.

Jim Dear and Lady brought Tramp home and he became part of their family. Soon he had his very own license. But he didn't mind one bit—it meant he could always be with Lady.

By Christmas, Lady and Tramp had four puppies of their own. With wonderful friends and a loving family, Lady and Tramp lived happily ever after.

DISNEY's
THE ARISTOCATS

O'Malley Saves the Day

In a grand house in Paris there lived a lady named Madame Bonfamille who had an elegant cat named Duchess and three kittens: Berlioz, Toulouse, and Marie.

But these were no ordinary cats. They were very civilized. Each day, the kittens had art and music lessons. "So you can grow up to be lovely, charming ladies and gentlemen," Duchess liked to say.

The cats loved their home. And they brought Madame such joy that she decided her entire fortune would go to them after she died.

"Cats?" the butler Edgar sputtered when he overheard Madame talking to her lawyer. "It's not fair!" He decided to get rid of the cats so the money would be left to him instead. As he warmed the cats' cream that afternoon, he mixed in some sleeping pills.

Duchess and her kittens lapped up the cream, and before long, they were fast asleep. Then Edgar put them in a basket and drove them far, far away.

When Duchess and her kittens awoke, they were in the countryside far from home.

"Mama! I'm afraid," Marie cried. "I want to go home!"

"Now, now, my darling," Duchess said. She tried to comfort her scared little kitten, but she was frightened, too. What would they do next?

The sky grew dark, and raindrops splattered against the ground. The cats ducked inside their basket.

"What's going to happen to us?" Toulouse asked, peering out at the storm.

Duchess drew her kittens close. "Darlings, I . . . I just don't know."

They were all alone.

Hours passed, and soon the dark skies brightened. Duchess stretched, then quietly jumped from the basket. The sun was shining, but they were still in a strange place, far from Madame and their friends Frou Frou the horse and Roquefort the mouse.

Here in the country, Duchess didn't know anyone. Then she met an alley cat named Thomas O'Malley. "Your eyes are like sapphires," he said smoothly, trying to charm her.

Duchess gazed at him. They were as different as two cats could be. Still, she liked the way O'Malley walked and talked. Could he be the friend they needed?

"I'm in a great deal of trouble," Duchess explained. "It is most important that I get back to Paris. Would you show me the way?"

"Show you the way?" O'Malley repeated with a laugh. "We shall fly to Paris on a magic carpet, side by side. Just we two."

Then Marie leaped out of the basket. "Three?" said O'Malley, eyes wide with surprise. Then Berlioz popped out. "Four?" And finally, Toulouse. "*Five?*"

O'Malley stepped back. "Well, now, ah . . ." He paused. "What I meant, you see . . ."

Duchess realized that the alley cat wasn't going to be the friend she hoped he'd be. She and her family began to walk away.

When they heard O'Malley shout, "Hold up there!" Duchess and the kittens stopped. A few minutes later, all five cats waited by the road as a milk truck drove toward them.

"One magic carpet, coming up!" O'Malley announced. "Step lively now!" He helped the cats jump onto the back of the truck, then said good-bye.

But as the truck started to drive away, Marie fell off of it. O'Malley grabbed her and leaped back on.

"Thank you, Mr. O'Malley, for saving my life," she said.

"No trouble at all, little princess," he replied.

Down the road, O'Malley whipped the cover off a giant container of cream. "Breakfast!" he cried.

But the driver caught sight of them in the rearview mirror and got angry. The cats raced off the truck, hurried through some tall grass, and ran up to a bridge with railroad tracks. They began to walk across.

"Be careful, children!" Duchess called to her kittens.

Clickety-clack! Clickety-clack! Wooo-wooo! A train was coming—right towards them!

Quickly, O'Malley pulled everyone onto a tiny platform beneath the tracks. They huddled together, holding on tightly as the train rumbled by. But as the bridge shook, Marie fell into the river below.

"Keep your head up!" O'Malley called. "Here I come!" He dove into the water and gently pushed the kitten onto a log.

Duchess leaped to the ground, then onto a branch that was hanging over the water. When the log floated past, O'Malley carefully tossed Marie over to Duchess.

He had saved the day once again.

That night, the cats reached the outskirts of Paris. "The kids are bushed," O'Malley said to Duchess. He led them to his place for some rest.

The abandoned house was old and run-down, a world away from Madame's mansion. Suddenly, music blared from the broken windows. O'Malley's friends were inside.

"Maybe we'd better find another place," the alley cat said. But Duchess didn't care how different everything was. It was all new and exciting, and she was certain O'Malley's friends would be just as nice as he was.

She entered a large room, where a group of alley cats were playing piano, trumpet, bass, and accordion. The room shook and furniture bounced. Soon, Duchess and her kittens were dancing to the jazz music and having the time of their lives.

Duchess looked around. She'd never met such cats or heard such music. And she'd never had such a dear friend.

Later, Duchess tucked the kittens into bed. She and O'Malley climbed out to the roof and looked up at the stars.

"Your eyes are like sapphires," he told her again. This time, he wasn't just sweet-talking. He meant it.

"And all those little kittens." He curled his tail around hers. "Duchess, I love 'em." He took a deep breath. "They need a . . . well, a father around."

"Oh, darling." Duchess sighed. She explained that she really wanted to stay with him, but that they needed to return to Madame.

O'Malley leaned close to Duchess. "I guess you know best, but I'm gonna miss you." He paused. "And those kids, too."

In the morning, O'Malley walked the cats home.

"I'll never forget you," Duchess told him tearfully.

"So long, baby." The alley cat padded away.

Just then, Edgar opened the door. He was surprised to see the cats again. Seconds later, he threw a sack over them and carried them to the barn. Then he tossed them in a trunk bound for Timbuktu.

Roquefort, the cats' mouse friend, saw everything. He raced after O'Malley. "Duchess! Kittens! In trouble!" he cried breathlessly.

O'Malley sent the mouse to get the alley cats, and then he raced toward the barn.

O'Malley pounced on Edgar, and the two tumbled about. The butler tried to run away, but Frou Frou the horse had him by the coattails.

Then Edgar's coat ripped and he was free! The butler and O'Malley faced off on either side of the trunk.

Just when Edgar seemed to be winning, O'Malley's friends burst into the barn. One dropped a harness over Edgar, and another tossed a bucket on his head. Roquefort quickly unlocked the trunk. O'Malley lifted the lid and Duchess and her kittens jumped to safety.

Then Frou Frou kicked Edgar, who tumbled into the empty trunk. The lid slammed shut, and the cats slid the trunk outside just as the mail truck arrived.

"This one goes all the way to Timbuktu!" the driver announced. He loaded the trunk onto his truck, and just like that, Edgar was gone.

Duchess and O'Malley looked at one another. After everything they'd been through, they couldn't bear to be apart. They meant too much to each other.

Madame understood. She was thrilled to have her beloved cats back and welcomed O'Malley into the family.

Three of a Kind

One day, a gorilla named Kala rescued a baby boy who was about to be attacked by a tiger. Even though he was human, Kala knew she loved the orphaned boy immediately. She decided she would be his mother, so she took him back to her jungle home and named him Tarzan.

The rest of the apes, however, didn't welcome Tarzan into their clan. Even after a few years, they couldn't see past the boy's hairless skin and narrow jaw. They never seemed to forget that although he could walk and talk just like them, Tarzan was not really one of them.

There was one ape besides Kala, however, who didn't mind that Tarzan looked different. Her name was Terk.

Whenever Tarzan was in trouble, which was fairly often, Terk tried to help him out—particularly with Kerchak, their leader, who thought that humans were dangerous.

Terk knew that none of her other friends wanted to spend time with Tarzan. So one day, when he asked to play with the apes, Terk told him he could—on one condition.

"You got to go get a hair," Terk said, "an elephant hair."

She knew that there was no way Tarzan would ever be able to do this. But he desperately wanted to fit in, so he decided to prove her wrong.

Before anyone could stop him, he dove off a cliff into the lagoon below and swam toward the elephants.

A young elephant named Tantor saw him. "Piranha!" he yelled, thinking Tarzan was a deadly fish. The other elephants paid no attention—until the boy grabbed one of their tails and yanked out a hair.

The elephants began a stampede, trying to escape. Terk was afraid Tarzan had been trampled. The ape frantically searched for her friend. She found him and pulled him out of the water. His eyes were closed, but Terk shook him till he woke up. As soon as Tarzan opened his eyes, he presented Terk with the elephant hair. Tantor was watching, and once he saw how harmless Tarzan was, he stopped being scared of him.

In the meantime, the other elephants charged through the apes' nesting grounds, nearly crushing the littlest ones.

Kerchak was furious. "What happened?" he roared.

"It was my fault," said Tarzan.

Terk thought Tarzan would tell on her and the others, too. But he didn't. "I'm sorry," was all he said.

Terk was impressed. But Kerchak wasn't. "He'll never be one of us," he angrily told Kala.

Heartbroken, Tarzan ran away.

Tarzan went to a river and knelt down at the edge of the water. He stared at his reflection. He realized that Kerchak was right—he really was different from the others. Then his mother appeared. She helped him to see that even though he didn't look like her, they were the same on the inside.

But Tarzan knew he had to show Kerchak he was just as good as everyone else. Tarzan decided to become the best ape *ever*!

Of course, it wasn't easy. It took years and years, and a lot of help from his old friend, Terk, and his new friend, Tantor. The three were inseparable. They helped Tarzan learn to swing on vines and find food. By the time he was fully grown, he was completely at home in the jungle. He knew how to do everything he needed to in order to survive.

217

Then, one day, a strange sound rang through the jungle. Tarzan grabbed a vine and swung through the trees until he arrived at the source of the noise. There he saw an odd-looking creature wearing clothes instead of fur. He was carrying a long tool with two holes at the end. Tarzan did not know that this creature was a man named Clayton, and that his tool was a gun.

Clayton was with other humans, and one of them was the most beautiful thing Tarzan had ever seen: a woman named Jane.

Although Kerchak warned Tarzan to stay away from the strangers, he was drawn to Jane. He learned that she and her father had come to study gorillas. Tarzan and Jane found a way to communicate, and he eagerly showed her around the jungle. Jane welcomed Tarzan to their campsite and told him about her home—a faraway place called London.

To Tarzan's surprise, he found Jane and he were more alike than he'd ever imagined . . . and before he knew it, he was falling in love.

His friend, Terk, was happy for Tarzan but worried, too. She knew that humans—especially the one called Clayton—meant trouble for the gorillas. She was soon proven right. Clayton captured Jane, her father, and Tarzan and locked them in the ship. Then, he began to trap as many gorillas as he could. He planned to bring them back to London and sell them to the highest bidders.

But Tarzan began yelling and Terk and Tantor heard him. "Tarzan needs us," said Tantor, "and we're gonna help him!"

They swam to the ship and with one heavy stomp, the elephant broke through the deck.

"Thanks, guys," said Tarzan as he and Jane and her father climbed out. Then, together, the friends hurried ashore to stop Clayton.

Clayton and his thugs had captured nearly all the gorillas and were loading them into cages when Tarzan swooped down on a vine, followed closely by the others.

Tantor grabbed the poachers with his trunk and flung them into the jungle, while Terk locked the men into cages.

As for Tarzan, he took on Clayton—man to man. Despite Clayton's knives and guns, he easily defeated him.

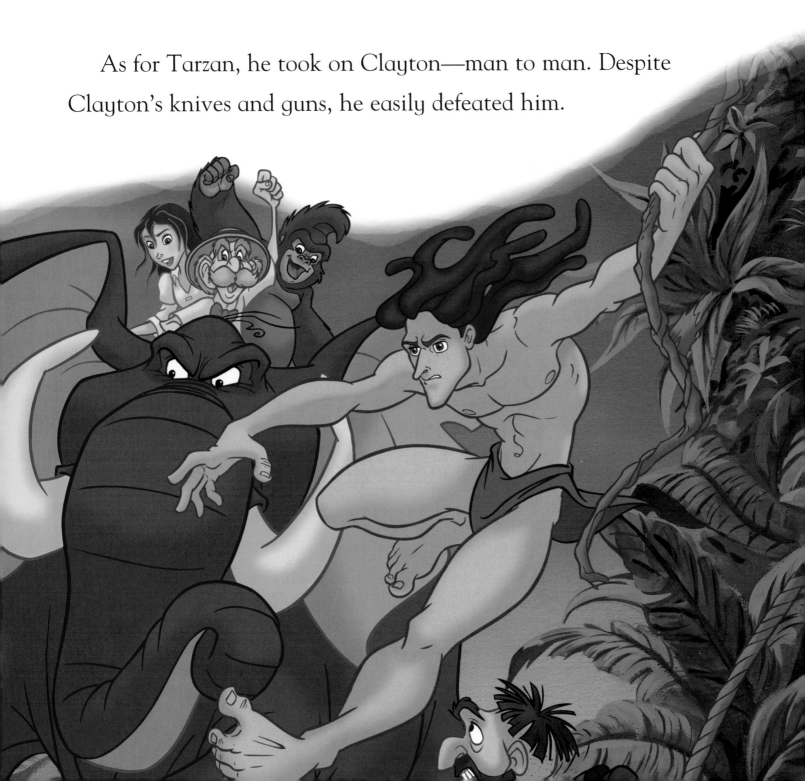

In the end, the poachers went back to England in chains, and Tarzan stayed where he belonged—in the jungle, with his best friends in the world . . . and Jane and her father, too!

"You have always been one of us," Kerchak told Tarzan gratefully.

And Tarzan knew that it was true—his friends had helped him to see that.

Disney's
THE
LION KING II
SIMBA'S · PRIDE

Enemies Become Friends

Simba, king of the Pride Lands, was nervous. He couldn't help worrying about his young daughter, Kiara. Today, for the first time, she would explore the area on her own. Simba knew that many dangers awaited her.

Kiara bounded from the den excitedly. But before she could scamper off, Simba stopped her. "I just want you to be careful," he warned.

"Okay, okay," the cub replied. "Can I go now?"

"Mind your father, Kiara," said her mother, Nala.

226

"Stay away from the Outlands," added Simba.

As Kiara left, Simba secretly sent Timon, a funny meerkat, and Pumbaa, a warmhearted but clumsy warthog, after her.

"Guys, I'm counting on you," the lion king told them. "Danger could be lurking behind every rock."

Kiara was fascinated by all the new things she saw. She ran through the fields and tried to catch a butterfly. But it wasn't long before she spotted something even more interesting: the Outlands, the area her father had warned her to stay away from.

Snap! Kiara heard a reed break nearby. Unfortunately for Simba, Timon and Pumbaa weren't very good at spying.

When Kiara saw them, she was angry. She ran away, and a few minutes later she met another lion cub. His name was Kovu. Together the two went exploring, with Kovu leading the way. The cubs frolicked and played and even had a close call with some hungry crocodiles.

The pair of lion cubs didn't realize that they were being watched—by both Kovu's mother, Zira, and Simba.

Simba was worried about his daughter's safety. He growled and leaped between the cubs. Soon, an angry Zira joined him.

Simba recognized the lioness immediately. His uncle, Scar, who'd died trying to kill Simba, had chosen Kovu as his successor. Because of that, Zira had plotted against Simba to make sure her son was the next lion king.

"I banished you from the Pride Lands," Simba told Zira. "Now you and your young cub, get out. We're finished here."

"Oh, no, Simba. We have barely begun," Zira replied ominously.

As Zira carried Kovu away, the cub locked eyes with Kiara. "Bye," he said.

"Bye," Kiara replied.

Time passed, and Kiara and Kovu didn't see each other. Kiara grew strong and sleek, but Kovu changed even more. Zira had trained him to hate Simba and the other lions of the Pride Lands.

One day, it was time for Kiara to go on her first hunt—alone. "Daddy, you have to promise to let me do this on my own," she pleaded.

Simba reluctantly agreed. But as Kiara left, he secretly sent Timon and Pumbaa after her. Simba knew that the Outsiders were watching, waiting for a chance to avenge Scar's death. He didn't want them to hurt his daughter.

As Kiara peered down the hill toward the plains, she spotted a herd of antelope. Her first hunt had begun! The lioness crept closer, then—*snap!*—a twig broke under her weight. Kiara watched as the herd took off, quick as lightning.

Determined, she tried again. But this time, she accidentally kicked some stones. Kiara stared helplessly as the animals ran away once more.

As the herd thundered by, Pumbaa and Timon tried to get out of the way, but not before Kiara saw them. She was furious!

"My father sent you!" she cried. Feeling betrayed, the lioness raced across the plains, as far away from Timon and Pumbaa as she could get.

Kiara ran toward the Outsiders' territory. Simba had been right to worry. Zira was setting a trap for the lion princess. She and the Outsiders lit the plains on fire, surrounding Kiara with flames. Soon, the young lioness collapsed, exhausted, in the grass.

Suddenly, another lion appeared and carried Kiara to a watery marsh, out of harm's way.

When Kiara opened her eyes, she was alone with the other lion. He seemed familiar to her, but still, she eyed him suspiciously. "Kovu?" she asked.

It *was* him—and he had saved her life!

Moments later, Simba arrived on the scene, and Kovu asked to join his pride, claiming that he had left the Outsiders. But in truth, Kovu had only one thing on his mind: getting rid of the lion king.

Because he had saved Kiara, Simba reluctantly allowed Kovu to return to Pride Rock.

From a distance, Zira gloated. She knew that as soon as Kovu was alone with Simba, he would kill him.

The next day, though, Kiara unknowingly interrupted the evil plan. Excited to spend time with her childhood friend, she persuaded Kovu to give her stalking lessons.

"Watch the master," Kovu said, "and learn."

Trying his best to show Kiara how it was done, Kovu raced up a hill, and pounced toward Timon and Pumbaa, who were shocked. The silly pair had been chasing a flock of birds who were eating all the best bugs.

Timon and Pumbaa asked them to scare the birds away. Kiara let out a loud roar and started running after them. Kovu followed, but he didn't understand. "Why are you doing this?" he asked.

Kiara laughed. "For fun!" she exclaimed.

Kovu had never done anything just for fun before. He roared along with Kiara, and they took off after the birds. Even Kovu was enjoying himself, until all of a sudden, they caused a rhinoceros stampede. The two lions ran in the opposite direction, along with Timon and Pumbaa. They all ducked into a small cave, laughing. Kovu had never had such a good time.

That evening, Kovu and Kiara lay in the grass looking at the stars. Kovu felt very close to Kiara, but he was torn by his loyalty to his mother. He didn't know what to do.

Just as Kovu started to walk away from Kiara, Rafiki, a wise baboon, appeared. He knew that Kovu and Kiara were meant to  be together and that they just needed a push in the right direction. He led the lions to a romantic place he called Upendi. Kovu and Kiara realized what was in their own hearts—they had fallen in love!

After the couple returned from Upendi, Simba noticed a change in Kovu. The next day, the lion king took him for a walk and told him the truth about Scar—how he'd taken over the Pride Lands by killing Simba's father, and then almost let the lions starve to death. "Scar couldn't let go of his hate, and in the end it destroyed him," said Simba.

"I've never heard the story of Scar that way," admitted Kovu. He couldn't believe how wrong he'd been! Kovu looked at Simba with admiration. He decided to make things right.

Just then, Zira and her followers appeared, ready to attack.

"No!" Kovu cried, but he was knocked unconscious.

The snarling lionesses chased Simba. Desperately, the lion king climbed a hill of loose logs, barely escaping the ambush.

Simba returned to the Pride Lands, hurt and exhausted. As Nala tended to his wounds, Kovu approached, only to be turned back by a mob of angry animals. All the inhabitants of the Pride Lands were sure that the attack on Simba had been part of Kovu's plan.

Kovu tried to explain, but only Kiara believed him. When Simba exiled Kovu from the Pride Lands, the lion princess followed him.

Soon, Kiara caught up with Kovu. "We have to go back," she said. "Our place is with our pride. If we run away, they'll be divided forever."

Kovu agreed. When they returned, the battle had already begun.

"This has to stop!" Kiara pleaded with her father.

Simba looked at Kovu and his daughter. He knew that Kiara was right and that they should choose peace over fighting. Even Zira's followers agreed. Zira, however, was still angry.

In a final attempt to kill Simba, Zira fell into a raging river. Kiara tried to save her, but Kovu's mother was swept away by the current, taking with her all the hate that had existed between the two prides.

The animals of the Pride Lands finally lived in harmony. Nala and Simba warmly welcomed Kovu's pride. Together with Kiara and Kovu, they rejoiced in the newfound peace across the land.

Disney's

ROBIN HOOD

Love Conquers All

One day, long ago, a beautiful fox named Maid Marian was playing badminton in the courtyard of Nottingham Castle with her lady-in-waiting, Lady Kluck. Nearby, a young rabbit named Skippy was practicing his archery. When one of the arrows flew into the courtyard, he went to retrieve it and bumped into Maid Marian.

His friends soon followed him. They hadn't seen Maid Marian up close before. "Gee, you're very beautiful," a small bunny named Tagalong said to her.

"Are you gonna marry Robin Hood?" another rabbit asked.

"Mama says you and Robin Hood are sweethearts," Tagalong piped up.

"That was several years ago, before I left for London," Maid Marian replied. Then she showed the children the tree in which Robin Hood had carved their initials. "He's probably forgotten all about me," she remarked.

Later, after the children had left, Maid Marian sat in the castle, thinking about Robin Hood. He was a dashing fox, and they had been in love, but then King Richard, a brave lion who was her uncle, had left to fight a battle. In his absence, his brother, Prince John, who was also a lion, had seized power.

The prince was very greedy and tried to get his hands on all the money he could. He even stole from the poorest members of his kingdom. But Robin Hood wouldn't stand for it. He stole money from the rich and gave it back to the poor. Prince John hated him and declared him an outlaw.

Marian glanced at the WANTED poster of Robin Hood that she kept in her room. Did he know how much she loved him? she wondered.

Meanwhile, in Sherwood Forest, Robin Hood and his bear friend, Little John, were doing chores in their hideout. Little John hung up clothing, and Robin Hood cooked dinner. But it wasn't long before the pot boiled over. The fox was distracted.

"You're burning the chow!" Little John cried.

"Sorry," Robin replied. "I guess I was thinking about Maid Marian again."

"Why don't you stop moonin' and mopin' around? Just marry the girl," Little John said.

"Marry her?" Robin replied. "What have I got to offer her? She's a highborn lady of quality. I'm an outlaw." But he couldn't stop daydreaming about her—he was in love.

A while later, a badger named Friar Tuck arrived. He told Robin and Little John about an archery tournament that the prince was holding the next day. Robin knew he could win the contest, but he didn't want to risk getting arrested.

But then Friar Tuck told him what the prize was: a kiss from Maid Marian. Robin Hood made a decision instantly. He would go to the tournament and win it—along with Maid Marian's heart. And somehow, he would do it without getting arrested.

The next day, Robin Hood and Little John disguised themselves and went to the tournament. Robin Hood was dressed as a stork and Little John wore a duke's costume. He walked right up to the Sheriff of Nottingham and said hello. When the Sheriff didn't recognize him, Robin Hood knew his plan would work!

Meanwhile, Maid Marian and Lady Kluck had arrived at the tournament. The beautiful fox had a feeling that she'd see Robin Hood.

"Oh, Klucky, I'm so excited," Maid Marian said. "But how will I recognize him?"

"Oh, he'll let you know somehow," Lady Kluck replied. "That young rogue of yours is full of surprises."

They made their way over to the royal box, where Maid Marian would be watching the tournament.

Marian sat on one side of Prince John in the royal box. On the prince's other side was Little John. He'd done such an amazing job with disguising himself that the prince thought he was the Duke of Chutney!

Soon, the archers paraded by the royal box. No one knew Robin Hood was one of them, not even Maid Marian. The outlaw went up to her and handed her a flower.

"It's a great honor to be shootin' for the favor of a lovely lady like yourself," Robin told her. Then he winked at her. "I hope I win the kiss."

Maid Marian realized who the stork really was. "I wish you luck," she said, "with all my heart."

The archers began to shoot. Robin Hood hit one bull's-eye after another. A few rounds later, only two contestants were left: the Sheriff and Robin Hood. The target was moved back an extra thirty paces. The Sheriff hit the target. Then, as Robin was taking aim, the Sheriff knocked into him with his bow to try to sabotage the contest.

The arrow traveled upward, but quick as a wink, Robin shot another arrow at the first one, which sent it down toward the target, and straight into the bull's-eye. It was so accurate that it even split the Sheriff's arrow in two!

Robin Hood had won the contest!

But as Robin Hood went to collect his kiss from Maid Marian, the prince figured out who he was. He used his sword to cut the fox's disguise away.

"Seize him!" Prince John ordered his men. "I sentence you to instant, and even immediate, death."

Maid Marian began to sob. "Please, sire. I beg of you to spare his life."

"Why should I?" the prince replied coldly.

"Because I love him, Your Highness," she replied.

Marian loves me! the fox thought. I have won her heart!

"My darling, I love you more than life itself," Robin Hood declared.

The beautiful fox was elated. Now she knew how he really felt.

But Prince John didn't care. He decided Robin Hood should die. Luckily, Little John was standing nearby. He held a dagger to the prince's back, convincing the ruler to free Robin Hood.

Then a fight broke out. The guards fought Robin Hood and Little John. Even Lady Kluck took part. She flipped the Sheriff over her head and onto the ground.

But Maid Marian got caught in the middle. Suddenly, guards were running toward her. "Help!" she called.

Robin Hood leaped up and grabbed onto a rope, swinging across the field to rescue his lady love. He swooped her up, and they swung toward the royal box, where he asked Marian for her hand in marriage. She accepted as he fought more guards.

Finally, they were able to escape, along with Little John and Lady Kluck. They all went back to Sherwood Forest, where they met Friar Tuck and the rest of Robin's band of merry men and celebrated with some dancing.

Prince John was very angry that Robin Hood had escaped. He decided to collect more taxes from everyone. When Friar Tuck wouldn't pay, he was thrown in jail. The prince sentenced him to death to lure Robin Hood back.

But the outlaw couldn't be caught that easily. He snuck into the prison and released the Friar and all the other poor folk. Then, he stole the prince's gold and gave it to the poor.

Eventually, King Richard came back and took over.

Because he was a just and fair king, everything in the kingdom went back to the way it had been, and Robin Hood no longer had to steal.

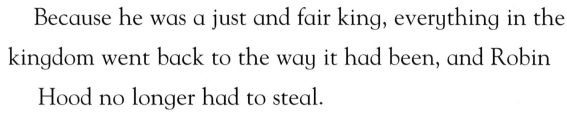

The king pardoned Robin Hood, which meant that he and Maid Marian could finally get married! All of their friends went to the ceremony. They had a wonderful celebration.

Marian and Robin couldn't have been happier. At long last, they were together, forever.

Disney
Winnie the Pooh

The Search for Tigger's Bounce

"Why, hello there, Tigger!" Winnie the Pooh exclaimed as his friend approached. Pooh, along with Piglet, Eeyore, and Roo, was standing on a bridge over the stream, playing Pooh Sticks. "Would you like to play with us?" the bear asked Tigger.

Tigger didn't seem at all interested. As he walked up onto the bridge, his shoulders were hunched over, his head drooped, and his tail dragged behind him. "Tiggers don't like to play Pooh Sticks on days like today," he said moodily.

Roo put down his stick and bounced over to Tigger's side. "What's the matter, Tigger?" he asked. "You don't look like your normal bouncy self."

Tigger shook his head. "No," he replied. "That's just the problem, fellas. I can hardly bear to say it—it's so horribibble. But I . . . I think I've lost my bounce!"

"Lost your bounce?" Roo said with a gasp.

"Oh, dear!" Piglet cried.

"I know the feeling," said Eeyore flatly. "I'm always losing things."

"What do you mean, you've lost your bounce?" Pooh asked.

Tigger shrugged. "The last time I bounced was yesterday," he replied. "But I haven't been able to bounce since!"

All the friends were quiet as they thought things over. "I know!" Piglet exclaimed. "We could all help you look for your bounce!"

Tigger sighed. "Thanks an awful lot, but I wouldn't even know where to begin."

Luckily, Roo had an idea. "When I'm missing something, Mama says I should try to remember the last time I had it . . . then start by looking for it there."

"All right, then," said Pooh. "Where was the last place you had your bounce, Tigger?"

Tigger scratched his head, thinking back. "Actually," he replied, "it was not too far from here." He gestured for his friends to follow. "Come on," he said. "I'll show you."

Pooh, Piglet, Roo, and Eeyore walked with Tigger along the bank of the stream. When they came to a place where the bank

fell sharply away and down to the water, they stopped. There, a large tree had fallen across the stream.

"I was just bouncin' along through the Wood, mindin' my own busyness," said Tigger, "when all of a sudden, I looked down to find that I was bouncin' on this here tree trunk, mighty high above the stream." Tigger paused, then added, "Don't get me wrong. Tiggers are good at bouncin' over tree trunks that are

mighty high above streams. They just choose not to."

At this, his friends all nodded sympathetically, so Tigger went on, "Anyways, when I got off that tree trunk, I wasn't in much of a bouncin' mood anymore. And I haven't been able to bounce ever since!"

His friends were quiet for a moment.

Then Eeyore spoke up. "You see what's happened, don't you?" he asked Tigger. "You had the bounce scared right out of you."

Tigger straightened up defensively. "Scared?" he said. "Tiggers don't get scared."

Eeyore corrected himself. "Did I say 'scared'?" he said. "I meant 'startled.'"

Tigger relaxed. "Well, yes, it was rather startlin'," he said agreeably.

"Well," said Roo, "if Tigger's bounce got startled out of him here, then it must be nearby."

"Let's look for it," suggested Piglet.

They all began to search for Tigger's bounce.

After a while, Pooh called to Tigger, "What does your bounce look like, exactly?"

"Exackatackly, I don't know," Tigger said. His already sad face fell a little more. "Aw, this is useless. We still don't know where to look, and we don't know what we're looking for."

The friends decided to see if Christopher Robin had any suggestions. They knew they could always count on him to look at a problem in a different sort of way.

When they found Christopher Robin, Pooh explained to him about their search for Tigger's missing bounce. Tigger added the part about the tree trunk and the last time he remembered having his bounce. Christopher Robin listened carefully. Then he took Tigger's hand and pulled him close.

"Tigger," he said, "you haven't lost your bounce."

"I haven't?" Tigger said, his face brightening.

"Of course not," said Christopher Robin. "Your bounce is not a thing that can go missing like . . . like Eeyore's tail."

"Lucky you," Eeyore said to Tigger.

Christopher Robin continued. "I think you got startled on that tree trunk. And then you got worried about bouncing. But you could never lose your bounce. You're a tigger!" With that, he gave Tigger a great big pat on the back. "And I know you could bounce right now," he added.

"You do?" Tigger said.

Christopher Robin nodded. "And everyone else does, too."

"They do?" said Tigger, looking over at Pooh.

Pooh looked up at Christopher Robin. "We do?" he asked.

"Yes, you do," the boy replied.

The bear realized Christopher Robin was right. "Yes, we do," he said, nodding his head.

Tigger looked at everyone. If his friends all believed in him, maybe they were right. A huge smile lit up his face. "Well, in that case," he said, "I do, too!" Tigger hopped a little hop, landed square on his tail, and began bouncing in place.

"Hey, fellas!" he exclaimed, overjoyed. "I'm doin' it! I'm bouncin'! And I'm still really good at it!"

"Hip, hip, hooray!" Christopher Robin cheered.

Pooh leaped in the air, and Piglet clapped with excitement.

Roo was so excited that he started bouncing high in the air, too. Soon, he and Tigger were bouncing their way around the tree.

"Let's see who can jump higher!" Tigger suggested. "Or faster!" He giggled. "It's so good to be bouncin' again, just like a tigger's supposed to."

"Oh, well," said Eeyore. "I guess you don't need to look for your bounce anymore."

The friends watched Tigger bounce. After a while, they decided to play Pooh Sticks again. But Tigger didn't go with them. He was too busy . . . bouncing and bouncing and bouncing.

Disney's THE LITTLE MERMAID

Sebastian Helps Out

Beneath the sea, all the merfolk gathered at King Triton's royal palace for a concert. Sebastian the crab, the court composer, was excited for everyone to hear his new symphony. He gestured for the orchestra to begin playing.

Everything went very smoothly until a large seashell opened. Ariel, the king's youngest daughter, was supposed to emerge from the shell and begin to sing. She had a lovely voice, and it was always a treat to hear her. But when the shell opened, it was empty!

King Triton couldn't believe his daughter hadn't shown up.

Sebastian couldn't believe it, either. The concert was ruined!

Ariel was busy exploring a sunken ship with her friend Flounder. She had completely forgotten about the concert. She finally remembered and swam straight home.

King Triton was furious when he found out where she had been. He believed that humans were dangerous. "I am never, never to hear of you going to the surface again!" he warned.

Ariel swam off. King Triton turned to Sebastian. "Ariel needs constant supervision," he said. "And *you* are just the crab to do it."

Sebastian was speechless. He didn't want to look after Ariel, but he couldn't refuse the king. He sank down in his shell, muttering to himself. "How do I get myself in these situations? I should be writing symphonies, not tagging along after some headstrong teenager."

That day, Sebastian began keeping an eye on Ariel. He followed her and Flounder to her secret grotto. It was filled from floor to ceiling with human objects that she had collected from sunken ships. He hid and listened quietly as the young mermaid sang about her dream to be part of the human world. He was so shocked that he lost his footing and fell off a ledge.

Ariel realized that he had been following her. "What is all this?" Sebastian exclaimed. "If your father knew about this place . . ."

The mermaid begged Sebastian not to tell King Triton. But just then, a ship sailing overhead caught her attention, and she began to swim toward it.

"Ariel?" the crab called. Then he realized she was swimming toward the surface.

"Jumping jellyfish!" he shouted.

"Come back!"

By the time Sebastian and Flounder reached the surface, a hurricane had begun, and the ship was sinking.

Ariel had rescued a human and was pulling him to shore. The human's name was Prince Eric, and the mermaid thought he was very handsome. He was everything she had ever dreamed about! Because the prince was unconscious, Ariel stayed by his side, even singing to him. But when she heard his servant coming, she dove into the water. She didn't want anyone to know she was a mermaid. She watched with Sebastian and Flounder as the prince awakened and returned to the palace with his servant.

Sebastian knew that King Triton would be very angry if he found out what Ariel had done. "We're just going to forget this whole thing ever happened," he told Ariel and Flounder.

279

But Ariel couldn't stop thinking about Prince Eric.

Sebastian tried to reason with her. "Will you get your head out of the clouds and back in the water where it belongs?"

More than ever, Ariel wanted to be among humans. The crab couldn't seem to convince her that life under the sea was better than life in the surface world. Then, by accident, he revealed to the king that Ariel was in love with a human.

King Triton was furious. He went to see his daughter at once. "Have you completely lost your senses?" he bellowed. "He's a human. You're a mermaid!"

"I don't care," Ariel said defiantly.

The king raised his trident and destroyed all of Ariel's human objects. After he left, Sebastian tried to apologize.

"Just go away," the mermaid said, sobbing.

Sebastian felt awful.

Ariel's crying was cut short by the arrival of two wicked eels who worked for Ursula the sea witch. They led the mermaid to their boss's cave. Sebastian and Flounder followed them.

Ursula offered Ariel a deal: she would give her human legs in exchange for her voice. "I will make you a potion that will turn you into a human for three days," the sea witch said. "If the prince kisses you before the sun sets on the third day, you'll remain human permanently. But if he doesn't, you'll turn back into a mermaid, and you'll belong to me!"

Ariel knew it was her only chance to get to know Prince Eric. Reluctantly, she signed her name to the contract. Moments later, Ursula had captured the mermaid's voice in a shell and transformed her tail into two human legs! Sebastian and Flounder rushed over to help Ariel. Now that she was human, she couldn't stay underwater for very long.

When Ariel made it to the rocky shore, she was greeted by another one of her friends, Scuttle the seagull.

Sebastian was beside himself. "This is a catastrophe! What would her father say? I'm going to march myself straight home right now and tell him!"

Ariel shook her head at him, since she had no voice.

"Don't you shake your head at me, young lady!" said Sebastian. Then he smiled hopefully. "Maybe there's still time. If we could get that witch to give you back your voice, you could go home

with all the normal fish and just be . . . just be . . ."

The little mermaid looked at him pleadingly.

Sebastian sighed. "Just be miserable for the rest of your life," he finished. He knew he couldn't turn his back on his friend. "All right. I'll try to help you find that prince."

Ariel was so thrilled and relieved, she gave the crab a kiss.

"Boy, what a soft shell I'm turning out to be," Sebastian said.

Scuttle located some rope and sailcloth with which to make a dress for Ariel.

Before long, Prince Eric found Ariel. Although she couldn't speak, Eric was still enchanted by her. One afternoon, he took her for a boat ride in a lush lagoon. Sebastian helped create a romantic mood by getting the lagoon's creatures to sing and play music.

But just as the prince was about to kiss Ariel, their rowboat tipped over! Ursula had sent her two eels to make sure Eric and Ariel didn't kiss.

Through a magical glass ball, Ursula watched Ariel and Eric topple out of the boat. "Nice work, boys," she said to the eels. "That was a close one."

But Ursula was still worried that the prince might kiss Ariel before sunset the next day. So she formulated a wicked plan: she would turn herself into a pretty young woman named Vanessa. Then she would use Ariel's voice, which was locked inside the shell on a cord around her neck, to sound like the little mermaid and win the prince's heart.

That evening, Vanessa went ashore and sang to Prince Eric. He was captivated—she sounded just like the girl who had rescued him. When Vanessa put a spell on him, the prince insisted that they be married the very next day.

Ariel was brokenhearted when she heard the news, but there was nothing she could do. She had no idea that Vanessa was really Ursula in disguise.

The next day, Ariel, Flounder, and Sebastian were sitting at the dock when Scuttle flew up. He explained that he had seen Vanessa looking in a mirror, and her reflection had revealed that she was really Ursula!

Ariel and her friends knew they had to stop the wedding. Sebastian cut a barrel loose and said to Flounder, "Get her to that boat as fast as your fins can carry you! I've got to get to the sea king!" He told Scuttle to stall the wedding.

Ariel hung onto the barrel as Flounder pulled it toward the ship. When she got there, Scuttle yanked the shell from Vanessa's neck. Ariel got her voice back and the spell on Eric was broken. But before they could kiss, the sun set and Ariel turned back into a mermaid. Vanessa transformed into Ursula and dragged the mermaid underwater. Prince Eric didn't want to lose Ariel, so he fought the sea witch in a fierce battle and won.

Although Ursula had been defeated, Ariel was still a mermaid. She couldn't live in Prince Eric's world.

King Triton saw how unhappy his daughter was. "She really does love him, doesn't she?" he said to Sebastian.

The crab nodded.

"Then I guess there's just one problem left," said King Triton.

"What's that, Your Majesty?" asked Sebastian.

"How much I'm going to miss her," King Triton explained. Then, with a flash of golden light from his trident, he gave Ariel human legs.

Sebastian was truly happy for Ariel. He would miss her, too, but he was sure they'd see each other again, soon.

Walt Disney's
Bambi

The Winter Trail

One winter morning, Bambi the young deer was dozing in the thicket when he heard a thumping sound nearby.

"C'mon, Bambi!" his bunny friend, Thumper, cried. "It's a perfect day for playing."

Bambi got up slowly and followed Thumper through the forest. It was a beautiful day! The sky was blue and sunny, and the ground was covered in a blanket of new snow. Icicles glistened on the trees.

"Look at these tracks!" Thumper said excitedly. He pointed to a line of footprints in the snow. "I saw them on the way over. Who do you suppose they belong to?"

Bambi couldn't guess, so they decided to follow the trail. They pranced and hopped through the snow. Before long, they came to the tree and saw someone who might have left the tracks.

"Wake up, Friend Owl!" called Thumper.

The bird peered down at the animals. He had only just flown to his favorite tree branch and fallen asleep. "Stop that racket!" he replied crossly and closed his eyes.

Bambi and Thumper giggled. Friend Owl was always grouchy when they woke him up.

"Friend Owl, have you been out walking?" Bambi asked.

"Now why would I do that?" Friend Owl replied, opening his eyes. "My wings take me everywhere I need to go."

Bambi and Thumper continued on.

Soon, they met up with Bambi's friend Faline. "You can help us find out who made these tracks," said Bambi, pointing to the trail.

Thumper thumped his foot impatiently. He wanted to keep going.

Faline nodded and began to walk with them.

Thumper hopped ahead quickly. Maybe their friend Flower the skunk wanted to come, too.

But Flower was hibernating. Thumper's mama had told him that meant the skunk would be sleeping all winter long.

When Thumper tried to wake Flower, the little skunk just mumbled, "See you next spring," without even opening his eyes.

The three friends decided to keep going without him.

Thumper bounded ahead. He followed the footprints to a frozen pond and glided across. "Come on!" he called. "There are tracks over here, too."

So, Faline and Bambi started to cross the pond. Before long, Faline had joined Thumper on the other side. But Bambi wasn't a very good skater. His legs went out from under him, and he fell on the ice.

"Aw, Bambi, come on," Thumper urged. "We can go skating later. I'll even show you how to spin around."

After a lot of slipping and sliding, Bambi finally took a running start and sped across the pond on his belly.

Next, the three friends walked up a snowy hill. At the top, they spotted a raccoon sitting next to a tree trunk, eating some red berries.

"Hello, Mr. Raccoon," Faline said. "Did you happen to see who made these tracks in the snow?"

But the raccoon's mouth was so full he couldn't say anything. He shook his head and began tapping the tree.

The friends looked around. Then they heard a "tap, tap, tap" in the distance.

"I know!" Thumper cried. "He thinks we should ask the woodpeckers."

"Oh, thank you," Bambi said. The raccoon waved good-bye as the friends headed toward a row of pine trees.

The tapping got louder and louder. Soon, Bambi, Faline, and Thumper had found the woodpeckers. The mama was pecking away, and her three children were sitting in holes in the tree trunk. They stuck their heads out when they heard Thumper cry, "Helloooooooo!"

The mama bird stopped her pecking. "Yes?" she asked.

"Well, you see," Bambi began shyly, "we were wondering . . . that is, we're looking for—"

"Aw, for Pete's sake," Thumper interrupted. "Did you make the tracks in the snow?" he called up to the birds.

"No, we've been here all day," the mama bird answered.

"Yes, yes, yes," her babies added.

Just then, Faline noticed that the trail continued. "Thank you," she called to the birds.

She rushed ahead, while Bambi and Thumper walked slowly. "If the tracks don't belong to the woodpeckers, and they don't belong to the raccoon, and they don't belong to Friend Owl, whose can they be?" Bambi asked his rabbit friend.

"I don't know," Thumper replied, frustrated.

They soon reached the end of the trail. The tracks led all the way to a snowy bush, where a family of quail was resting. "Hello!" Mrs. Quail cooed as the deer and rabbit approached.

"Did you make these tracks?" Thumper asked her.

"Why, yes," Mrs. Quail answered. "Friend Owl told me about this wonderful bush. So this morning, my babies and I walked all the way over here."

Thumper and Bambi nodded. Then Thumper pointed to the edge of the glen. Faline was there. "Mrs. Quail invited us to join her for a snack, so I was just getting some leaves," she said. The three friends sat down to eat with the quail family.

But the sun was getting low, and the friends had to get home. They'd spent all day following the trail! When they turned to leave, a big surprise was waiting for them—their mothers!

Bambi bounded over to his mother and stretched his nose up for a kiss. "We've been looking for you," she told him tenderly.

Thumper was surprised. "How'd ya find us?" he asked.

Thumper's mama said, "Well, your sisters pointed us in the right direction and then. . ." She looked down at the deer and rabbit tracks that the three friends had left in the snow.

"You followed our trail!" Faline cried. Her mother nodded.

"Now, let's follow it back home," Bambi's mother said.

And that's just what they did.

Now the most popular Disney Storybooks have a new look!

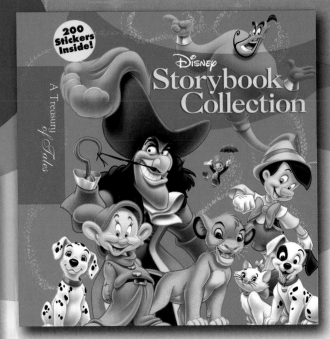

Disney
Storybook Collection
200 Stickers Inside!
A Treasury of Tales

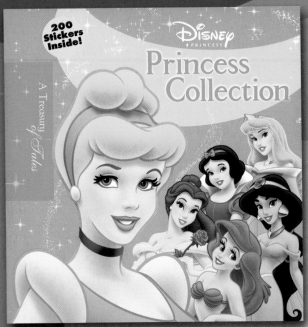

Disney PRINCESS
Princess Collection
200 Stickers Inside!
A Treasury of Tales

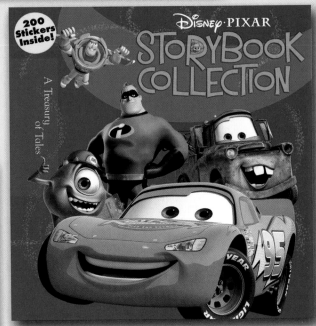

Disney · PIXAR
StoryBook Collection
200 Stickers Inside!
A Treasury of Tales

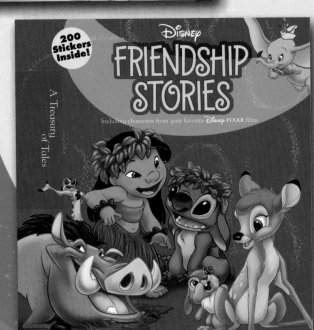

Disney
Friendship Stories
200 Stickers Inside!
Including characters from your favorite Disney · PIXAR films
A Treasury of Tales

200 Stickers in Each Book!